PUBLISH
& PERISH

This Large Print Book carries the
Seal of Approval of N.A.V.H.

PUBLISH
& PERISH

SALLY S. WRIGHT

Thorndike Press • Thorndike, Maine

This book is a work of fiction. With the exception of Ben Reese and recognized historical figures, the characters in this novel are fictional. Any resemblance to actual persons, living or dead, is purely coincidental.

Published in 1998 by arrangement with Multnomah Publishers.

Thorndike Large Print ® Christian Mystery Series.

The tree indicium is a trademark of Thorndike Press.

The text of this Large Print edition is unabridged. Other aspects of the book may vary from the original edition.

Set in 16 pt. Plantin by Al Chase.

Printed in the United States on permanent paper.

Library of Congress Cataloging in Publication Data

Wright, Sally S.
    Publish & perish / Sally S. Wright.
       p.   cm — (Ben Reese mystery series ; 1)
    ISBN 0-7862-1566-6   (lg. print : hc : alk. paper)
    1. Large type books. I. Title. II. Series : Wright, Sally S.
Ben Reese mystery series ; 1.
    [PS3573.R5398P83 1998]
    813′.54—dc21   98-27445

Because of John Reed,
who went in on June 5th
and came out under a Piper Cub

List of Characters

Walter Buchanan:	farmer who boards Ben Reese's horse
Ed Campbell:	Ph.D. candidate, Alderton University
Jim Cook:	president, Alderton University
Howard Ellis:	dean of men, Alderton University
Craig French:	English professor, Alderton University
Grace Giardi:	French professor, Alderton University
Bernard Greene:	English professor, Alderton University
Chester Hansen:	chief of police, Hillsdale, Ohio
Waldo Hubbard:	anthropology professor, Ohio State University
David Krause:	anthropology professor, Ohio State University
Maggie Parsons:	Ben Reese's housekeeper/tenant
Sally Poole:	student, Alderton University

Ben Reese:	archivist, Alderton University
Rena:	student in Bernard Greene's apartment
Sarie:	Richard West's first secretary
Nancy Shaffer:	Richard West's second secretary
Doug Smith:	student, Alderton University
Clarence Watson:	porter at Deniston Hall
Albert Weber:	maintenance man at Alderton University
Richard West:	chairman, Alderton's English department
Ellen Winter:	Ben Reese's new archives apprentice

CHAPTER ONE

Friday, November 18, 1960

It was two in the morning in Oxfordshire, England, when the call came through from America that woke Clarence Watson, the porter at Deniston Hall.

When he told the story later, he always referred to it simply as "the call," once he knew what it had led to, as though it were the only call in all of human history.

Some of those in the village said it was a "dereliction of duty" that he'd been in bed to begin with, but Clarence claimed (and the director supported him) that he was expected to retire, once his duties at the research institute had been performed.

And they had been, with some precision. He'd locked the doors for the night and extinguished the lights, for all the research fellows were in and in their rooms. They rarely kept late hours or indulged in even a whisper of unbridled behavior. They were established scholars, of settled habits, who studied the lives and the writings of men and women who were long dead and turned to dust.

And Clarence wondered why, when he had time. Aged laundry lists were pored over. Musty receipts were copied. One of the fellows was even counting the number of times Shakespeare had written the word "nature," for all the good that would do anyone, then or later. But the fellows were usually pleasant. And Clarence enjoyed his work.

The night the call came, he'd wound the tall clock on the staircase and checked to be certain the stove was turned off and the windows were locked in the kitchen. He'd gone into the dining hall and the Fellows Lounge to see that the candles had been put out and the fires properly banked, before he examined the ash trays and the wastepaper baskets. The fellows smoked continually and made a great nasty smell wherever they went, and Clarence had found more than one basket in flames during his years at the institute.

But all was in order when he stepped into his own rooms off the front hall — the office first (with the telephone and the mail slots and the log book), and then on through to the bed-sitter where he had his daybed and his telly.

He always made a point of mentioning, when he told the story at The Black Swan (and he told the story of Ben Reese frequently, whether he was asked to or not), that he hadn't watched television at all the night "the call" came. He'd had a bit of a headache and had lain down at twelve, after his last young gentleman came in from Oxford from some sort of "do" at Magdalen College.

It felt like the phone was ringing in his head when it went off, and Clarence was none too pleased. In fact, he jumped out of bed and snatched up the receiver in a bit of a temper.

Gladys White was on the exchange that night, and she was quite excited to have a call all the way from America. There weren't many in those days. It was terribly expensive, and the connections were generally poor.

Clarence was afraid later that he'd been a trifle testy with the American caller. But at the time, he was unsympathetic, and he made quite a point of saying that it was two o'clock in England, whatever time it might be in any other part of the world. The American gentleman replied just as pointedly that he fully understood that, and he wouldn't be calling if it weren't an emergency.

It was then that Clarence Watson saw where his duty lay. He rushed up the stairs in

11

his slippers and robe without bothering to alter his attire, though he did make certain that his robe was well closed and his sleeping dress properly concealed.

He seemed to be wheezing a bit, more than he would've expected, certainly, as he hurried up the carpeted stairs, stepping cautiously on the six or seven treads that creaked more loudly than the others.

He didn't wish to disturb any of the other fellows as he summoned Dr. Reese, and he knocked on the door as quietly as he could. Even so, Benjamin Reese answered after the first rap and called to him to come straight in.

Dr. Reese had clearly been asleep, and he squinted painfully as he turned on his bedside lamp. But he sat up against the headboard straightaway. And it was then that Clarence saw the scars on his upper body. They were old and well healed, but terrible nevertheless. A jagged gash curved across his left ribs, and there were several round indentions (which Clarence knew to be bullet holes, having worked in a hospital in the First War) spattered over his arms and torso. There was one very long and deep incision that ran through the well-developed muscles of Dr. Reese's left arm and up around his shoulder toward his back.

But Dr. Reese made no attempt to cover them. He just asked Clarence why he'd wakened him and if there was anything wrong.

"A call's come through for you from America and the gentleman says it's an emergency."

It took Dr. Reese no time at all to leap out of bed, throw a robe over his undergarments, and start down the stairs toward the phone. Much less time than Clarence would have believed. Though he'd seen it in the last war. The way Americans rush everywhere they go.

"Richard! . . . Yeah, I can hear you." Ben Reese was standing in the small, paneled telephone booth at the bottom of the stairs, holding the receiver in one hand and his robe closed against the cold with the other. "What's up? It's not your heart, is it? . . . Good, that's a relief . . . Oh, yeah? . . . Wait a minute, what act of treachery? . . . What do you mean the culprit's put in an appearance? . . . Richard, you can't just say 'I can't explain now'! Tell me what you meant about incriminating someone! . . . So? . . . You're sure? . . . OK . . . All right . . . You've got your pills, I hope . . . Good, because it sounds like you've lost your temper . . . Fine. I'll wait for you to call tomorrow."

Ben Reese stared at the receiver before he dropped it back into its prewar cradle. Then he smiled and shook his head and said, "Thanks a lot, Richard!" in disgust.

Yeah, but you know he wouldn't call in the middle of the night if it weren't important. And he wouldn't get off the phone without a reason, either. But why couldn't he just say what he had to say and stop beating around the bush?

Because he's Richard. And digression's become a way of life.

By the time Ben wandered into the Fellows Lounge and took a book down off the fiction shelves, the first death had been accomplished. He realized that later — when he had reason to think about it.

He also saw, by the end of the investigation, that if Richard West had remembered to tell him the day he left for England what he, Richard, had decided to do, all of the deaths and most of the suffering might have been prevented.

Thursday, October 27, 1960

It had been a long day for both of them, the day Ben left for England. A clear, cold, typical fall day in central Ohio that started before dawn. Long before Richard leaned

14

his fingertips together under one of his chins and said, "That would be a noble pursuit!" And it would certainly serve a useful purpose. More than my own novel, obviously.

He'd been typing for quite a while at the long pine worktable in the library half of his living room, surrounded by books and old moldings and bare wood floors. And he'd just stopped to watch the thin pale strip of gray at the edge of the earth while he talked to himself, and lit his pipe, and retied the cotton rope that was holding his blue flannel robe together across his sedentary stomach.

I know there'll never be a better time to take on too many pursuits. Because whether I like it or not, procrastination becomes a luxury when you have a heart condition and you're middle-aged.

And yet I wonder why it never occurred to me before? More importantly, I wonder if I still have it. Yes, there's the proverbial rub. For if I don't, who would?

He pulled the paper out of his typewriter and slipped it into a three-ring binder. But he didn't snap the rings together then the way he intended. "Rats, I've forgotten the croissants!"

They hadn't risen as much as he'd been afraid they would, and he tossed half of them in the freezer and arranged the rest on a cookie sheet while he thought about where to start. There was a kind of childlike concentration on his soft round face as he poured his third cup of coffee and asked himself what he would've done with it. He might have put it with his papers in the living room, but he doubted it. And he knew it wasn't on the bookshelves there, or in the bedroom.

He tried to remember when he'd last seen it, and what state it had been in then. It wasn't bound, he knew that. It was either in a folder or a large manila envelope, so the guest room made the most sense. And it was easier to get to than the attic.

He started with the closet full of cardboard boxes — the articles and essays and the drafts of his books — and found papers by students he'd forgotten he'd kept. He picked one out of a pile and read part of a page, and then sighed to himself as he put it back. "Sad, really. David Krause." Failing a course that should have been easy for him. For this is an essay that should have been published.

It was surprising, too, that he still had it. Although he also found an odd assortment of mementos from every college he'd attended. And all of it would be useful when

16

he started the novel. He'd need scraps of real life to remember what school was like.

But the manuscript he was looking for wasn't in the closet. So he stretched himself up to his considerable height of just a hair under six-feet-five and pulled down the stairway to the attic without having to get a stool.

It wasn't in his army footlocker. Or the big metal trunk he'd had since boarding school. And it wasn't with his Christmas decorations either, which was no surprise. All that was left was a cedar closet full of clothes he'd outgrown but couldn't bring himself to throw away.

And that meant that if he still had it, it was probably down in the boxes on the guest room shelves in a place that made no sense. He'd have to go through everything meticulously in irritating detail, including all his graduate students' papers, and he didn't have time to do it just then.

He flipped the stairs back up into the ceiling, and adjusted the rope around his robe. Then he took one large manila envelope into the library, where he lay down in his big black Victorian dentist's chair and began to look at pieces of his past.

He guffawed once or twice in his deepest voice and said, "My word, I was thin," before he sneezed. He stared at one photograph for a long time, as though it hurt to study it as much as to put it back. And then he picked up the poetry he couldn't remember writing.

The sky had turned a pale salmon pink when Richard stuffed the last yellowing paper inside the envelope and rubbed his hot, grainy eyes with his index fingers.

He'd probably given it back years ago and forgotten all about it. But if he hadn't, it was in with something totally unrelated and he'd look for it later, after he'd taken Ben to catch his plane. He could also wait till the weekend if he wanted to. There was no real reason to rush. And it was time to set the table in the dining room.

Richard usually looked forward to company, but this time he sighed as he dug out two place mats and the family silver. It was too early in the morning for barbed remarks and buried agendas.

Still, he popped the croissants in the oven and got the butter out to soften.

And then he caught a glimpse of himself in the bathroom mirror as he was dropping his robe on the floor. The look on his face was exactly what it usually was — disgusted and appalled and resigned at the same time.

About the time Richard West was adjusting the water in his tub, Ben Reese was standing on his own back porch a mile and a half away in boots and britches and an old canvas hunting jacket, holding a bridle and a dressage saddle. He was tallish and thin, and he could almost have been a college kid himself — standing there watching the wind in his neighbor's field, thinking that the soybeans looked ready to take out.

Someone was burning leaves over toward Sutter Road and it smelled ridiculously good. And yet he knew he ought to go in. His housekeeper was up. The lights were on in her apartment, so it had to be later than he thought.

He'd just dropped his saddle on the rag rug by his breakfast table, when Maggie opened her stairway door and stepped into the hall on the other side of his kitchen. She took a basket of wash back into the laundry room and then said, "Just as I thought!" as she brushed past Ben's refrigerator in her long wool robe.

"I wanted to ride Journey one more time, and I couldn't see when else I was going to fit it in today."

"That's because you think more about your horse than you do your health! The rest of the world sleeps and eats, you know. Or have you forgotten?"

"No, I'm performing a community service. You wouldn't know what to do with yourself if you didn't have me to worry about." Ben was grinning at her with his eyes crinkling at the corners, while he balanced on his bootjack and pulled off a mud-splattered boot.

"Maybe. I'd probably start pestering my grandkids. 'Course, I don't think most people under forty know how to take care of themselves. They haven't seen enough of what life can do."

Ben Reese had done behind-the-lines reconnaissance from Omaha Beach past Remagen. And he'd left his wife, dead, on a metal bed in a county hospital. But he didn't say anything.

And Maggie looked away. "Don't pay any attention to me, I'm just talking to hear myself talk. So what do you want for breakfast?" She was opening the refrigerator door, while patting her wiry gray hair the way she always did in the morning after she'd taken off her net.

"I'll just have coffee and a glass of juice. I've got to get cleaned up, and then get the new archives apprentice started. It's too early to call her now, but don't let me forget, OK?"

"You can't fly to England with nothing in your stomach!"

"I'm eating lunch with Richard."

"So?"

"OK, Maggie. You can fix me a tomato sandwich if it'll make you feel any better."

Ellen Winter was cold and she wished she'd worn a coat, but she was also curious about Ben Reese, and she might not get another chance to see his house. It had to be the one on the hill, just before the open field, if she'd gotten the directions right. The old brick Victorian farmhouse with chimneys and porches and bay windows shooting out like quills on a porcupine.

Ellen was trying to train herself to be observant, because eventually she wanted to be a writer. She was just reaching for the twist bell, while studying the carving around the door, when the door opened unexpectedly, and a small, solid-looking, gray-haired woman in an apron smiled and waved her in. "My land! You must be chilled to the bone without a jacket!"

"It wasn't this cold in town."

"It's the wind. We're the first thing it hits when it's coming out of the west. Want me to find you a sweater?"

"No, I'm OK. Thanks."

21

"Dr. Reese is eating breakfast, so I'll have to take you into the kitchen."

"Is that one of his paintings?" It was a big canvas, and it was much looser and more savage than she would have expected, the same way the inside of the house was lighter and emptier and more contemporary.

Whoever the woman was, she'd disappeared through the archway to the right of the door, and Ellen followed her across a lean white living room into the dining room beyond.

"I guess he painted it three or four years ago."

"Does he ever sell them?"

"No, it's just a way to pass the time. 'Course I like pictures that look like something myself." She was talking over her shoulder, carrying a Boston fern and a watering can toward the sink in the brick-walled kitchen.

"Hello, Dr. Reese."

"Thanks for walking over, Ellen. It's given me time to get organized." Ben Reese was sitting at a butcher block table by two tall narrow windows, eating what looked like a tomato sandwich. There was a saddle in a chair beside him, and a pair of riding boots on the floor leaned forward at a funny angle.

"I didn't know you rode." Ellen sat down

opposite Ben and tried not to stare. She was beginning to feel awkward and it made her mad.

"Before I forget, this is Margaret Parsons. She has an apartment upstairs, and she keeps house for me part-time. Maggie, this is Ellen Winter, my new apprentice. If you finish the journals while I'm gone, Maggie can give you as many more as you want."

"Sure, just give me a call."

"Do you remember where I left that pile of papers I had last night?" Ben was looking at Maggie over the top of his glass of milk.

"They were on the coffee table last I saw. I'll go hunt for 'em! You sit still and eat your breakfast."

"Thanks, Maggie." Ben smiled to himself. And it looked to Ellen like he was about to say something else and then decided against it, as he stuck a piece of bacon back inside his sandwich.

"Anyway, in answer to your question, yes, I do." His hair had slipped down his forehead like a patch of weathered wheat, and he was sliding his spoon from one hand to the other, while he gazed out the window at a gray and white bird eating sunflower seeds upside down.

Ellen sat in silence on the other side of the table, staring at the index finger of his left hand. It was sticking straight out as though he couldn't bend it, which she found strangely disconcerting, partly because she hadn't noticed sooner. And then she saw the scar, snaking across his palm and running up the underside of his wrist. "I'm sorry, what did you say, Dr. Reese?"

"I thought you asked if I rode."

"Ah. Yes."

"I've got an old racehorse, and I'm trying to learn dressage twenty years too late. Good! Thank you, Maggie. Would you like a cup of coffee, Ellen, or a piece of toast?"

"Just coffee, thanks." Ellen was still freezing. She stretched her wool skirt over as much of her legs as she could, and tucked her hands under the bottom of her sweater.

"I'm going up to my place, Dr. Ben, unless you need me."

"Thanks, Maggie. I'll talk to you this afternoon before I go." Ben slid Ellen's coffee over to her, and then he leaned back and propped his chair against the wall. "So while I'm in England, you're going to start my archivist's crash course —"

"I know what I wanted to ask you! Oh, I'm sorry. I didn't mean to interrupt."

"No, go ahead."

"I work for the student newspaper, and it occurred to me the other day that since you

24

and Dr. West and President Cook all went to Indiana University, it might make a good feature article if I interviewed the three of you. You know, find out how you all ended up here, and how you feel about big universities like Indiana, in comparison to small private schools like Alderton. But with you going to England, I thought I ought to see if you were willing to do it, and then arrange the interviews."

"I take it you're desperate for copy." Ben laughed and reached for an apple.

And Ellen dropped her eyes and tried not to look taken aback. "Not really."

"I'm sorry, it's too early in the morning to joke around. But if I were you, I think I'd start with Dr. West. Although you'll have to give President Cook quite a bit of advance notice, for him to be able to fit you in."

"So I can interview you too, when you get back?"

"Sure. Anyway, archivists never know enough, and when I got here, I had to evaluate all the artifacts that had been stuffed in the basements of five university buildings . . ."

Ellen watched him as he talked, concentrating on the wide mouth and the strong jaw, partly because it seemed strange to her that he'd be interested in antiquarian objects

25

— in books and coins and historical documents. She'd expected someone elderly and effeminate to be in his position. Even though that was just the kind of preconception she tried to avoid. Ben Reese was probably in his late thirties and he looked like a normal person. And then she realized she hadn't been listening and hoped he hadn't noticed.

"So I had to research all kinds of strange things I'd never thought about. Chandeliers, for instance. Lucy Webb Hayes gave us two after she redecorated the White House." He laughed and popped at least a quarter of a sandwich in his mouth. And then he studied Ellen silently for a minute.

Ellen looked at the detachment on his face, at the large gray eyes that seemed to be evaluating her too impartially, and she began to feel like a piece of complex machinery.

"But first you have to start with the basics, and I want you to do some library work on diplomatics."

"I don't know what that is."

"The study of documents. Read some general information and see where it leads. Then look at paleography, which is basically the study of ancient and medieval handwriting. You'll have to learn something about the history of printing and paper-making too. Watermarks are especially important."

26

"Why do you study things like that?"

"Because archivists have to be able to distinguish between false and genuine documents. And to do that, you also have to be knowledgeable about writing materials — parchment and papyrus and wax tablets. Now, don't panic. I don't expect you to do any of this in depth. I'm just trying to give you a very quick overview of what an archivist does. You'll understand as you get into it."

"I hope so."

"Then after I get back, we'll begin painting restoration and identify a few coins. Now, on the top of that pile, you'll find a land grant. It's nothing rare or valuable, but it's written on vellum and signed by . . . ?"

"James Madison!"

"What's the first thing you'd do to authenticate it?"

"Check the dates, I guess. Try to find out if he was in a position to issue a grant like that at the time?"

"Good! Then what?"

Ellen's hair was pulled back in a braided ponytail and her straight black eyebrows had tightened toward her nose, and her whole face seemed to be concentrating. "I don't know enough to guess. Are there resource books that cover something like that?"

"Everyone alters the style of their signature in the course of a lifetime, so you'd compare this one to authenticated ones of approximately the same date. If the style is substantially different, it's a forgery. Of which there were many."

"So how long do you think you'll be gone?"

"I might be back by Christmas, but it'll probably be the middle of January."

"And you're sure you'll still have time to work with me?"

"I wouldn't have taken you on as an apprentice if I didn't think I'd have time. All this sabbatical means is that I don't have to go to committee meetings, and I can work on my own research instead of everyone else's." He stacked his dishes in the sink and looked out into the back across the fields. "Is it still cold out?"

"Yeah, I should've worn a coat."

"Then the least I can do is give you a ride down to campus. Let me get my keys and grab a jacket."

"Hi, Sarie."

"Oh, Dr. Reese! I didn't expect to see you again!" Richard West's secretary was smiling softly at Ben as she pushed her small, black, almond-shaped glasses up off the end of her nose. Her thin, dyed, damaged hair was standing in a circle around her head a little like a dandelion that's gone to seed, and it probably made her face look plumper than it really was.

"I told Richard I'd bring these books over, and I need to leave a message for him too."

"He's in class right now. Oops! Wouldn't you just know? I won't be a minute, I promise!" Sarie answered the phone in a self-effacing whisper, which Ben always thought of as her little-girl-actress-of-the-thirties voice, while he looked at his watch and thought about leaving a note.

"There! Now what can I do for you, Dr. Ben?"

"These are for Richard." He'd already laid three books of Blake's poetry and engravings on the end of her desk, and he'd begun to turn toward the hall door. "He can take them back to Janie when he's done. And if you'll tell him I'll pick him up here for lunch about one, I won't take time to write a note. Thanks a lot, Sarie. I have to run, I've still got some packing to do."

"Wait, Dr. Ben, please!" She sounded almost panicked.

And Ben asked himself again why he sometimes let her indecisiveness become an irritation. "What, Sarie?"

29

"Here at one? Or at his house at one? If you haven't already talked to Dr. West, I want to be absolutely sure I've got it right. Wait, let me get a pencil! OK. I'm ready!"

"At least Sarie gave you the right message this time." Ben was already seated by the brick wall, absently running his hand over the worn wooden beam beside the table.

"I wouldn't go so far as to say that." Richard West smiled as he dropped into the chair on the other side of the window, which overlooked the river and an old weathered water wheel standing gray and still in the sun. "There were three or four different versions, but 'office' and 'one o'clock' occurred more often than any of the other alternatives, and I stationed myself accordingly as an act of faith."

"Poor Sarie."

"She's a very nice person. It's a sentence I often mutter like an incantation."

The waiter arrived and they ordered without the epicurean fuss that eating with Richard sometimes entailed, which, from Ben's point of view, was something of a relief. They both watched the river, the narrow, quick-moving stream that gushed and darted over shale and small stones between banks of overhanging trees.

Then they talked about books and music while they waited, until Richard adjusted his brown tweed vest and said, "So what is it I need to know before you leave?"

"Well, first of all, I've given Walter Buchanan your number, so if anything happens to Journey, he'll call you."

"Fine."

"I told Maggie she could drive my car, so once you drop me off at the airport, you can take it back to her and she'll drive you over to your house."

Richard nodded.

"If there's anything that looks important in the mail, Maggie or Janie will bring it to you so you can open it and let me know."

"OK."

"I also have a new apprentice named Ellen Winter, and if she gets into a dither, I told her to talk to you too."

"I hope I'll be able to muddle through."

"Yes, somehow I think you'll manage. So what's up with you? You said you'd had a hectic morning."

"Craig French came to breakfast. But I'd rather not talk about that experience in the interests of charity and a well-digested lunch. You have a crumb stuck in the cleft in your chin."

"Thank you, Richard. Where would I be

31

without you? Didn't you have a meeting of department chairmen too?"

"Yes, and despite President Jim's well-intentioned and subtle leadership, it was the usual study in verbosity and self-aggrandizement and too little can't be said upon the subject." Richard looked at the tablecloth as though he were analyzing the caper sauce on his filet of trout.

Ben ate several spoonfuls of curried chicken soup. "So why do I have the feeling there's something specific you want to say?"

"There're several, actually, and I probably should have written a list."

"You? Richard West? The man who's committed all of western literature to memory?"

"You're being more obstreperous than usual!"

"Am I?"

"Yes, you are! And as I was *trying* to say, before I was so rudely interrupted, I've written my will, and I —"

"Why, all of a sudden?"

"It's not a matter of 'all of a sudden.' Everyone should, and I believe in doing these things with care and farsightedness."

"But you're feeling all right?" Ben was looking at Richard's large person — his huge hands and his round head and his very tall, rather portly body — as though illness or fear should be visible if he studied him carefully enough.

"There's no reason to be alarmed, Benjamin. The angina seems to be under control. But it has forced me to contemplate certain inevitabilities which most of us would prefer to ignore. And that's rather a good thing. We need to acknowledge the transient nature of this world, and contemplate the kingdom of God, and evaluate our own priorities."

"Absolutely."

"But the reason I mention it, is that I've made you the executor of my will. I've also made you several bequests, and some of them are rather amusing."

"You're giving me your two brass lamps from the Salvation Army!"

"Yes, as a matter of fact I am, and don't be flippant! I'm also giving you my Russian icon, which you, at least, will be able to appreciate."

"Thank you, Richard. I hardly know what to say."

"I'd rather you wouldn't say anything, to tell you the truth. Besides, I started another undertaking this week, which I think you might find interesting." Richard paused significantly.

Ben thought he looked rather pleased with himself. "Well? Are you going to tell me or not?"

"I've decided to write a novel. Now, please don't laugh, Benjamin! I have no delusions about my abilities in fiction, but I thought it would be great fun to try my hand."

"Good for you! That took me by surprise."

"I thought it might." Richard was smiling endearingly, his soft rosy face shining with suppressed enthusiasm. "I'm only just beginning to put together a loose-leaf notebook of plot ideas and character sketches, but my greatest fear at this stage is that I won't be able to manage the dialogue and description."

"Nobody knows till they try."

"Exactly."

"Where does it take place?"

"Academia, needless to say. What else could I possibly write about? It's all I know in such lamentable detail."

"Is it OK to ask what it's about?"

"It's not formulated enough for me to discuss the plot itself, but I'm hoping to illustrate what it's like to finally become a professor, and then face the vicissitudes of educating the young amidst all the controversies in today's institutions. Though I intend, of course, to write a serious novel, not a piece of sociopolitical propaganda."

"Good, because that's deadly."

"One thing I do want to make extremely clear is that I have *no* intention of telling anyone else that I'm working on a novel. I may make a complete hash of it —"

"Yeah, right."

Richard held up his hand. "And even if I don't humiliate myself in the attempt, I don't wish to discuss it with anyone else."

"I won't say anything. I promise. But I think we better ask for the check."

"I know there's a particular reason you drive this ancient vehicle" — Richard was lighting his pipe while rolling down the passenger window of Ben's 1947 Plymouth — "but I can't remember what it is."

"My brother restores old cars and he gave it to me for practically nothing."

"It isn't what it used to be, you know. My mind. Age, Ben. It has its way with all of us." Richard was clenching his pipe in his teeth and pulling his coat collar up against the wind.

And Ben watched him gaze into the distance the way he would if he were really feeling morose. "Richard, you are forty-three years old, and your brain is as remarkable as it ever was. Even if you did start acting like a middle-aged professor before you were thirty." Ben laughed.

But Richard didn't. He grunted inscrutably while he hunted through his pockets for another book of matches. "I was only curious, you understand. There's no reason to take umbrage."

"I wasn't!"

"I'm actually rather fond of your car. It's unusually comfortable for a person of my proportions. And of course I know, Benjamin, even as I speak, that though you would never refer to anyone's personal excesses, you would be greatly relieved if I were to regain the boyish physique I once took for granted."

"Now wait a minute —"

"When you were a lowly undergraduate, I might add, and I was responsible for your intellectual attainments!"

"I didn't say a word!"

"Of course you didn't. You never do." Richard smoothed the sides of his sleek auburn fringe (the top having receded and thinned to a length that would never again be whipped in the wind). "You don't believe you have a right to influence anyone else's behavior."

"You're sure about that, are you?"

"Though naturally I, with my temperament, have never understood it. But I suspect that's why you fought advancement. Particularly as an Army Ranger."

"I had enough trouble looking after myself."

"So you've always said. And yet you were a reconnaissance expert who captured German command posts, deciphered their documents, and predicted their movements across France, Belgium, and Luxembourg, which was one of the most arduous assignments that —"

"I know what I wanted to ask you. What happened when you had breakfast with Craig French?"

"You don't seriously think you can change the subject so cleverly that I won't notice, do you!"

"No, but if I couldn't hear the humor in your voice, I might think you were a pompous person!"

"Really? What could possibly make you think that?" They looked at each other and laughed, until Richard said, "Never mind. We will leave the invasion of Europe in the dust of the recent past. As to the tiny professor . . ." Richard picked at his pipe, knocking the tobacco onto the road before placing it in the side pocket of his disreputable rain-coat with a flourish of supreme contempt. "Is the elephant discommoded by a wayward flea? No. And I didn't let Dr. French provoke me."

"You're sure?" Ben said it dubiously and laughed as he looked at Richard.

"And neither did he reintroduce the disgust he feels at my appointment as chairman of the English department —"

"Since that is, after all, old news."

"*And* because it was a request that led him to seek me out. You see, it was his protégé — the twit, the callow youth, the ubiquitous lounger, Bernard Greene — whose form can be observed through the front window of Patsy's Bar and Grill at any hour of the day or night, who was the impetus behind little Craig's visit. It seems that our Dr. French, in the darkest recesses of his shriveled soul, is convinced that Bernard has already shown himself to be more than deserving of tenure."

"Why? Why does French support him?"

"They share the same contempt for the values of civilized society."

"Except that Bernie acts, and French sneers from the sidelines."

"I couldn't have put it more aptly myself."

"And so you restrained yourself, did you?"

Ben was pulling out onto the first four-lane highway they'd seen on their way north from Hillsdale into Columbus. "When he told you Bernie deserves tenure?"

"I believe I ventured to say that next to the travesties of such organizations as the Teamsters Union and the civil service, tenure is responsible for much of what is wrong in our crumbling society. One should rise and fall upon one's accomplishments, not be given safe asylum!" Richard slid down, settling himself loudly against the soft gray seat, and folded his hands upon his large brown vest.

"Well? I'm sure you didn't stop there."

"No, I went on to point out that although I may have to award tenure from time to time against my will, I have never met a less likely candidate than the odious Bernard. Not only is he unable to scan the horizon unaided, to say nothing of the prosodic structure of Milton or Donne, but also, left to his own devices, he would abandon all the great writers of western civilization in order to concentrate on Burroughs, Ferlinghetti, and Kerouac!"

"That's a depressing thought."

"He has also gone so far as to trifle with the glandular systems of at least one undergraduate. And without putting too fine a point upon it, Bernie is an unprincipled wart! I didn't express myself in quite those terms, but I expect Dr. French understood my position."

"You do make yourself abundantly clear. And while I'm thinking about it, and can fit it in, I want to know exactly how you've been feeling since you saw the doctor. I'd like a real answer, Richard. I do not want to be sidestepped on this."

"I think I'm doing quite well, actually. Though I don't expect to live forever. Nor would I wish to. Not in this world, at any rate."

"Didn't your father have a heart condition too?"

"Yes, he was making a house call on a polio patient when he died of angina at forty-five. But mine seems to have stabilized rather nicely."

"You're sure?"

"Yes. And while I'm thinking of it, give me the number of this research institute of yours. I have an envelope in here somewhere." Richard began searching his pockets with his enormous fingers, as a small, pleased expression settled on his large pink face. "A Godiva chocolate wrapper, as it happens, but it should suffice nobly."

"Let me give you Walter's number too.

His son, Joey, is going to ride Journey, and I —"

"Remember how Jessie and you and I used to swim in Walter's quarry? . . . Ah, Benjamin. Of course you remember! Now give me his number and be done with this infernal horse of yours!"

They drove awhile in silence, watching the fall woods and the fields and the curving roads that took hills and valleys in quick, narrow turns. Because no matter how much both of them might have regretted it, the mention of Ben's dead wife in superficial conversation made an awkwardness between them that Ben didn't know how to avoid. Richard had done more to get him through it than anyone else could have. But Ben still couldn't talk about it. Not casually. Not in offhand remarks. And once he started discussing it seriously with Richard, he wouldn't be able to stop until he'd gone on so long he found it embarrassing, even if Richard didn't.

"So what do you think of the presidential campaign?"

Richard was calmly wiping his forehead with a large cream-colored handkerchief, and when he snorted, the report was oddly muffled. "Is that what it is, this study of form without content? Nixon 'emphasizes what's good in America,' while John F. Kennedy rides a mule in Sioux City!"

"I know. It's pathetic."

"It's the arrogance that takes one's breath away. Papa Joe makes his millions in bootleg liquor, and then grooms his eldest son from the proverbial cradle to become president of the United States. Only to decide, when the boy dies, that the second son will do in a pinch, even though he's a habitual philanderer like his father. Did you know Joe Kennedy told Churchill after Dunkirk that the only option left the British was unequivocal and immediate surrender?"

"Yes, I did, as a matter of fact."

"Which is not to say I admire Mr. Nixon. No, I wouldn't trust either one of them to do my grocery shopping!"

"Bearing in mind that you do take your grocery shopping seriously."

"Very amusing, Benjamin. I wish *I* could laugh. Where are the statesmen in either party?! It's enough to make me grind my teeth!"

"I know. It's a national embarrassment. But you are beet red, and there's a vein pulsing in your temple, Richard, and that can't be good."

"Don't worry, Benjamin. I do not intend to give the liberal left the pleasure of my death yet. Nor any time in the foreseeable future!"

"Good! Glad to hear it."

"You're not heading toward the short-term lot?"

"There's no reason for you to wait till the plane leaves, and I told Maggie you'd be back about five."

"Why is it she's using your car?"

"Hers is falling apart."

"Ah."

"Thanks for bringing me, Richard. Even though you do make it hard for me to adjust to British reticence."

"You'll manage. Admirably, I might add, with your temperament. Take care of yourself, Ben."

Ben stood on the sidewalk with a bag in one hand and a briefcase in the other, and watched Richard pull away from the curb, pipe smoke rolling across the interior like a black cloud, while the muffler rumbled as he whipped the Plymouth into second gear. The sight of Richard in a hurtling machine reminded Ben of something, but he couldn't think what. Toad and the motorcar? Almost, but not quite. Winston Churchill hijacking the train during the Boer War.

"Benjamin!" Richard West was backing

up at a remarkable rate and rolling down his window at the same time. "I knew there was something I meant to tell you! I've been considering another rather interesting enterprise and I wanted your opinion!" The car behind him honked and Richard glared over his shoulder. "Ah, well. 'There is nothing more dreadful to an author than neglect, compared with which reproach, hatred, and opposition are names of happiness.' I'll write! Either that, or we'll talk when you get back. It's nothing that can't wait!"

Ben waved and watched him thunder off, thinking, He won't write. He hates personal letters. He can't stop editing and it drives him nuts. And why did he suddenly quote Samuel Johnson?

There wasn't time to ask, because by then Richard was shooting into third, heading toward the cloverleaf that took him back to Hillsdale.

CHAPTER TWO

Friday, November 18

Richard was humming the "Hallelujah Chorus" while weaving in and out of Columbus traffic, and he almost missed the entrance to the Columbus Zoo. But he caught himself at the last moment and swept between two closely parked cars.

He muttered, "Popcorn boxes, bubble gum wrappers! You wouldn't find that in Zurich, no indeed!" while he negotiated the parking lot, carefully avoiding the stickiest deposits, and deciding as he went, to start with the big cats. He began to wonder if it wasn't masochism on his part. They were so flea-bitten and depressed looking, shut in their ugly cages with the insensitivities of ignorant humans perpetually before them.

He then considered the elephants. But they were no better off. So he watched the pygmy hippopotamus, who at least seemed to enjoy holding his breath underwater in his small, fetid tank.

The afternoon was winding down and the wind was turning colder, and Richard swept into the humid heat of the aviary as though it were a pleasure he'd been postponing.

He crossed the main room, fingering his pockets for the wooden ring Ben's father had carved for him, while a hundred different bird calls echoed against the high tile walls. He stood quietly for a moment in the tall trees at the back, and then he threw the wooden piece above his head.

Before it hit the floor, a black tern swooped over him and caught it in his beak, dropping it at Richard's feet like a retriever. "Hello little guy! That was very good! Ready? Here you go!" There were three other black terns backpedaling above him, hovering the way they fish above a salt marsh, holding their positions more patiently than most people wait for a table.

"You could kill them doing that! They could choke and swallow it or something!"

Richard turned and looked down upon a short, stringy, middle-aged woman, who suffered from fallen arches and a penetrating voice. "I have been relieving the boredom of birds of this sort since the age of ten, and I've carefully designed this ring to keep such a catastrophe from occurring. But since you obviously find my behavior upsetting, I shall leave you to your own devices." Richard nodded and walked away from her more briskly and with more coordination than someone as tall and heavy as he usually does.

I shall go in search of Bert! I wonder why they decided to move him? Richard was humming one of Wagner's arias as he examined the cages on both walls, never noticing how many people he passed turned and watched him with uneasy eyes. Of course that's the trouble with *The Ring*. Once you get Wotan in your head, he's there for the day. Though I'm sure Wagner would have been an infuriating fellow to know, in spite of his gifts and abilities.

Which leads me to consider other treacherous characters and nefarious acts, because someone must have taken it. And why anyone would is a very interesting question.

For what else could've happened to it? I certainly wouldn't have thrown out my own copy. And I've searched every conceivable spot at home and at the office. I've talked to all the logical people, and none of them has seen it. And though I shall wait to make an accusation until there's incontrovertible evidence, it certainly looks to me as though . . . Ah! There he is, in the corner cage. "My own favorite blue-mutation Panama Amazon parrot! Look at you, running back and forth on your little limb. What a display of enthusiasm! You may be a mutation, Bertie, but you're very beautiful. You still remember your name, don't you?"

"Bye-bye, big boy!"

"Now-now-now! Your name is Bertie, remember?"

"Hello-o-o. Hello-o-o!" The bird used a playfully rising and falling inflection, and watched Richard intently out of one large eye. "What-cha-doin', big boy?"

"You're trifling with me, aren't you, Bertie? Because you can say Bertie, can't you? Come on. Say Bertie for me. Please."

"Hello, Bertie. What'cha doin'?"

"Very good! Tenses aren't important, are they? No. And only an individual as remarkable as you would remember the name of a famous composer. You remember, don't you, Bertie? Ludwig von Beethoven."

Bertie cocked his head and looked dubiously at Richard, whose face was inches from the pale blue bird's. "Good-bye. Good-by-y!" Bertie said it very expressively and Richard laughed.

"Come on now, Bertie. I'll say it very slowly. Ludwig — von — Beethoven! Ludwig — von —"

"Why am I not surprised to find Richard West talking to a parrot!" It was a cold, brittle, sarcastic male voice.

Richard turned to face a tall, broadly built man with a red beard and a wide flat face, who looked like he was in his late thirties.

He was watching Richard West with his mouth stretched contemptuously to one side and his head tilted straight back. "So Dr. West doesn't recognize me! Gee, that's a real disappointment. And it's gotta be a lot harder for me. You must've put on fifty pounds."

"Your face is familiar, but I . . . weren't you at I.U.? Yes, of course! You're David Krause."

"So I did make an impression! Good, that makes me feel better. Was it when I dumped the garbage on your lawn? Or when I threw the rock through your window?"

"It was your essay on the Indian tribes of North Dakota. I'd hoped to be able to publish it in the literary journal the English department had just introduced." Richard said it calmly, his large face carefully neutral, his eyes straightforward and painstakingly polite.

"You don't quit, do you? No, you're so civilized, and so analytical. You *never* make a decision without evaluating the precedent you might be setting."

"Don't I?"

"No, because Richard West doesn't get emotionally involved. Not with anyone. Especially students. Even if they're going through hell!"

"How can you generalize with such assurance?"

"I suppose you *might*. Maybe. If it was one of your little protégés."

"Why do you assume —"

"My mother *died!* The entire family was falling apart, but you wouldn't bend your stupid rules once! No, Richard West has to maintain his standards. Because standards are more important than people. Right?"

"As I recall, Mr. Krause —"

"*Dr.* Krause!"

"Ah! Dr. Krause! Good, I'm glad to hear it. You failed your first semester too, from what I remember, before any family problems arose. You actually gave the impression of being far more interested in fraternity activities than you were the classroom."

"Oh, well, pardon me! The only college freshman ever to get sidetracked by too many parties!"

"The fact that it's a common occurrence doesn't mean it should be condoned, does it? Not from my perspective. Not when one is trying to prepare students to be productive in later life."

"So you know how to put old heads on teenage bodies?"

"No. But I think character is developed by being bruised by reality, day after day."

"How can you still think in platitudes after all these years?"

"Also, from what I remember, the Indian paper was the only assignment you turned in the entire second semester. Yet you were clearly capable of doing the work, for you got an A on that essay, and it was one of the few I gave that term."

"I bet that must've hurt —"

"No, it was actually a pleasure."

"— seeing someone who wasn't a sycophant get a decent grade."

"I disagree completely with your analysis. But, of course, you knew that already."

"I'm almost surprised you remember."

"I remember your essay very well."

"Did you ever think about giving me extensions?"

"I did! I remember distinctly that I —"

"Only on that essay. That's why it was the only one I handed in. But do you face the results of your decisions?"

"I beg your pardon?"

"Did you ever even wonder what happened to me? Did you!"

"Well, I —"

"I could only go to college because one of the customers in my dad's grocery had taken an interest in me and paid my tuition. Of course, after *you* got through with me, she lost interest, not too surprisingly. And I had to go home and butcher beef for a year and a half before I enlisted."

"Is that my fault?"

"Oh, no! No, of course not. Richard West never makes a mistake!"

"I know I tend to be —"

"Ironic, isn't it? Twenty years later, out of the blue, I see you talking to Waldo Hubbard in the hall at O.S.U. But only because I could go to school on the GI Bill. No thanks to Richard West."

"You followed me this afternoon all the way from Ohio State?" Richard's face was flushed, but his eyes didn't falter, and his voice was smooth and restrained.

"Oh, yeah. You bet. I wouldn't miss a chance to have a chat with Richard West. You don't teach at O.S.U.?"

"No. Alderton University in Hillsdale."

"I work with Waldo Hubbard now. I'm an associate professor in the department of anthropology. But not so I can do to other kids what you did to me! No, you're the example I use when I look in the mirror in the morning of what I *don't* want to be."

"I didn't enjoy it. I thought you had a great deal of ability. I was trying to find a way to help you want to use it."

"Were you! I don't think so. I think that's

what you tell yourself in your empty house. It is empty, isn't it? No wife. No kids. Yeah, I can see it in your eyes. Richard West. Eating at a silent table. Overeating might be a better word. Sleeping in an empty bed. Right? No one-night stands for Richard West! The man who lectures parrots who can't talk back!"

Richard didn't say anything. He stood and stared at David Krause, at the cold, clear hatred in his wide hazel eyes.

"You won't be alone now, though."

"No?"

"Not anymore. Now that I know how to find you, you can bet I'm gonna stay in touch!"

Street lights were burning along the walks on the Alderton campus while the wind shook the trees, turning pools of light into intricately scattered patterns. There were a few people holding their coats and tucking their heads toward their collars. But it was Friday night, and there weren't many going back to work in offices, and labs, or in the library.

Richard West was one of the few, and he was trudging across campus (in his threadbare raincoat and hand-tailored three-piece suit) with an enigmatic expression on his face and a pipe stuck in the corner of his mouth.

I realize, of course, that one can't have everything one's own way. But it's getting so I can't even stay in my own home in the evening without being pursued. I suppose it's not her fault, really. Not entirely. The world conspires against the weaknesses in us all.

Weakness. Yes, there's a concept that applies to one and all. Mine, of course, are legion, and usually spring from either pride or self-absorption. Yet David Krause's animosity does seem a bit extreme. Though I suppose he has some cause if I didn't give him extra time as often as I thought.

Even so, he should've known he couldn't pass, handing in only one assignment out of fifteen or more. And yet he didn't know, apparently. And it's unsettling, the depth of his dislike. Still, I'm to blame as well. His mother had died, for heaven's sake, and it was obviously a severe blow. I should have checked to see how he was getting along.

I am glad I at least called tonight and tried to extend an invitation. There seemed to be a hint of a thaw when I told him I was sure Ben would be glad to see him too. Odd, though, that David would actually ask if Ben had bought a horse.

And why, I ask myself, did I decide to

walk?! It's much colder than it was an hour ago. Yes, so why don't I just pop along in here, and get warm on my way out the other side?

Richard opened the west door of the glass and steel History Building and walked east through a long, empty hall. He lit a match as he came around a corner, and was raising it toward his pipe, when he saw a pair of women's loafers, two feet above the floor, sticking out past the end of the wall that stood facing him on his left.

He tiptoed toward them on his rubber-soled shoes and came upon a student couple, fully clothed and lying on their sides, on the bench beside the door to the Religious Life office.

"Ah-hah!" Richard used his deepest, most powerful voice and the surprise effect was wonderful. "This is not the sort of activity one expects by the Religious Life office!" Both of them were bolt upright in the next two seconds, and there were clothes being straightened and overcoats buttoned, while the odors of hops and malt hung in the warm air. "Have you no sense of propriety! Have you no concern for other people's sensibilities? The beasts of the field have more natural modesty!" Richard wheezed asthmatically and whisked out a notebook while fixing his cold blue eyes upon them. "Much to my own chagrin, you have put me in a position of having to record your names!"

The tall, blond, curly haired young man (who reminded Richard of a Celtic warrior) gave his name carelessly, without fear or hostility. But the girl, who looked too young to be drinking any sort of alcohol, seemed defiant and embarrassed and somewhat the worse for wear, as she hesitated under Richard's gaze, and adjusted her skirt before answering.

He watched them weightily, shoving his notebook into his breast pocket, and then pointed toward the outside door. "You may depart into the outer darkness, but I would prepare myselves, if I were you, for a summons to those in authority!"

When he saw their breath streaming behind them in the cold night air, he chuckled to himself and lit his pipe, dropping the burned match in his coat pocket with all the rest.

Five minutes later, Richard unlocked his office door and turned on the overhead light. He threw his coat in the corner on a pile of books, before sitting down at his desk and rolling a sheet of paper into his electric typewriter with the unconscious ease of an expert. He'd once been a military attaché, and he could type at least a hundred and fifteen words a minute, which had made more than one secretary insecure.

That night he composed a quick note, referring to his notebook to validate his spelling, before rumbling down the hall and stuffing it in a pigeonhole by the administration offices.

He gathered his own mail from across the hall and whistled his way back to his office, dropping everything else on his desk as soon as he'd read the label on a brown-paper package. He tore the paper off and read through the first few pages of a plainly bound blue volume, as he walked around his desk and threw himself in his sunken leather chair. He shouted, "That miserable, conniving, cowardly twit!" and cast the book on his desk, staring at it as though it were alive and dangerous and able to corrupt the flesh it touched.

He wiped his forehead with his handkerchief and began reading again, suspiciously, almost as though it were against his will. He dialed the phone and spoke a few brisk words before hanging up in disgust. Then he flung himself against the high back of his chair and sat staring at the wall, tapping his fountain pen on his front teeth.

He searched his desk drawer as though he'd come to a decision, and grabbed a piece of crumpled paper, smoothing it with one hand while he reached for the receiver. He spoke briefly and dropped it heavily into its black metal cradle. And then he lit his pipe impatiently.

He was staring at the telephone as though he could will it to ring, looking more and more indignant as each minute passed, as though he suspected he was being played false by powers in the outer world.

He was at the drinking fountain when it finally rang, and he ran panting back to his office. "Ben? . . . I need to speak to Dr. Reese . . . Of course I realize it's two in the morning in your part of the world, but I'm calling on a matter of urgency! . . . Thank you! Yes, I'll wait." Which he does, glaring at the clock across from his desk, until he shouts, "Ben! This is Richard. Can you hear me? . . . No, no, nothing like that! No, it's more surprising and far more upsetting. I've uncovered an act of treachery which demands some form of retribution, and you and I are probably the only two people on the face of the earth who can incriminate the guilty beast! Of course, I knew there was an unusual degree of ambition in this particular quarter, but it never occurred to me that . . .

Hold on just a minute, someone's at the door . . . Ah! Yes . . . Ben? The culprit has just put in an appearance and I'll have to call you tomorrow . . . No, I can't explain now, but you'll understand then, only too well! . . . Yes, I have my pills, and I've not lost my temper! . . . Yes, all right. I'll talk to you tomorrow!"

Ben sat in a small paneled booth, staring at a solid, respectable English phone, pondering the fact that he was now wide awake and was not going back to sleep. For one thing, the tall clock on the staircase was striking the chimes of Big Ben, while the house murmured to itself, heavy and slow and profoundly British, smelling of old books and polished wood and dusty draperies, creaking with age and the effects of the night air on antiquated ducting.

Ben apologized to Clarence, the porter, for the inconvenience he'd been caused, and wandered into the Fellows Lounge. He pulled *The Nebuly Coat* by John Meade-Falkner off one of the fiction shelves, before stirring up the ashes in the wide stone fireplace and throwing three small logs on the flickering coals. He took two pillows off the sagging sofa and settled himself in a chair by the fire, thinking, Richard's off on another campaign. But that's good. He usually accomplishes something and it keeps life interesting.

It was part of Ben's general philosophy to mistrust speculation, to think that toying with any hypothesis in circumstances like that, when he didn't have any real data, was an irrational waste of time and energy. So he opened his book and pushed Richard past the edge of his conscious mind.

And then he decided, twenty pages later, to visit Meade-Falkner's grave at the Norman church in Burford. He'd first go to the Evensong service, and then see if he could find it.

Jessie was lying on her side next to him with that bone strutting from the flesh of her hip like a white wing. Ben knew he was dreaming, but with the logic of the night, he was able to wish that he wasn't *and* that it would last, at the same time. Jessie stretched out beside him again, with her dark hair spread across the bed and her eyes watching him analytically, while she talked about one of her graduate students imposing Freud on *The Wind in the Willows*.

Her hand was moving down his side and she was sliding her mouth across his chest and smiling with her eyes. And then he was letting his lips drift down the length of her neck, following the curls of her ear like the chambers of a nautilus, hearing his own voice say, "Don't wake up. Please! Not now, not this time!" when his hand slipped underneath his head and he woke up in a flowered chair.

He'd never even heard the term *amniotic embolism* until she'd died of one. She'd gone into labor four months early, and a blood clot had floated away from the umbilical cord and hit her lungs. One second she was there. The next second she wasn't.

The baby had been too fragile to live. But Ben sometimes wondered why he didn't think about him more than he did. Probably it was because he'd never known him as an individual. He'd never had a voice or a personality.

There'd even been times since Jessie died when he couldn't remember her face when it was fluid. When she was talking or laughing or chewing on a pencil, making the small sounds people make that say more of what they think, sometimes, than words. She'd had an ability to concentrate so intently — grading papers, rubbing Sam's ears, digging up the dirt around her herbs. Ben used to watch her when she wasn't looking just so he could appreciate the foreignness of her, the ways in which she was separate and completely unlike him.

He had a handful of photographs, but none of them caught the quickness and the funniness and the twists of her mind. They hardly even caught her face. She'd hated having her picture taken. Because she hated being made self-conscious.

But the dream was hovering around him. And it was almost like she was there, like he could've heard her breathing, if he'd known how to listen. She used to come up to him anywhere, when he was shaving or stacking wood or working on a painting. She'd tuck her arms under his and kiss the hollow between his collar bones, because that's the way she was and he was there.

It got stronger the whole time they were married, the fusion between them. And even though she'd talked about it easier than he had, she'd known what she meant to him. He'd never gotten any of her letters, because he was moving too fast, but she'd had his all the way across Europe. Maybe that was part of why they'd been the way they were. They'd had to wait so long with so little chance of living to enjoy it.

She used to follow his scars with her index finger, winding around his ribs, up his left arm and across his back, then down the inside of his right thigh — letting it rest in the slick round holes. She kept him from wanting to hide them. She said they reminded her of abstract engravings, and they'd helped contribute to the uniqueness of his soul.

Ben laid his book on the floor, but he didn't get up and go back to bed. Why should he? What was there in any bed that could make a difference to him?

Saturday, November 19

The sun had burned off the mists in the high places of the Cotswold Hills, when Ben was awakened by the sound of voices in the residents dining hall. He took his time opening his eyes and surveyed his surroundings with detachment: the faded chintz sofa, the books on the high walls, the hunt scene over the mantelpiece, the mullion windows facing east — and the crick in his neck that was not going to go away soon.

He ended up feeling trapped that whole day while he waited for Richard to call back, even though there were accounts of the Moravian influence on John Wesley, and references to Disraeli he'd intended to study there at Deniston Hall.

It had been built overlooking the River Windrush by Sir Alexander Dermott (a member of Parliament and an opponent of

Disraeli's), who'd envisioned the establishment of a residential library for scholars of future generations.

And now they came from all over the world to stay in its modest rooms and examine its hundreds of thousands of printed pieces. It was close enough to Oxford to do research there as well. And the grounds themselves were beautiful. Ben loved the gentle laciness of the countryside, even as the soft green lushness turned into winter.

And yet for some inexplicable reason, everything he really felt like doing had to be done in Oxford; which was strange, because he usually waited well.

That day he was having to work at it. He was fighting an uneasy restlessness, tapping a metaphorical toe and staring at the soft yellow stone walls of Deniston Hall the way Richard had stared at his the night before. Probably. Because *patient* isn't the word I'd use to describe Richard waiting for a trans-Atlantic call.

But it wasn't until ten o'clock that night that Ben heard from Richard, and then it was indirect. The aged Clarence found him in the Fellows Lounge, drinking a cup of tea in front of the fire, and examining a reproduction of a Book of Hours that had belonged to Etienne Chevalier.

Clarence handed Ben a telegram, and turned away, collecting dirty ashtrays as he went.

Richard West died last night of a heart attack. Stop. Sorry Dr. Reese. Stop. Funeral Monday 1:00 P.M. Stop.
Ellen Winter

Sunday, November 20

It was a five-hour flight, followed by customs and another connection, but Ben had an aisle seat so he'd at least be able to stretch his legs. He opened the biography he'd bought in Oxford while the last of the passengers settled into their seats, only to find himself watching the man across the aisle wrap his fountain pen in layers of Kleenex as though it were a sacred act.

He was a small man who seemed to enjoy badgering the woman next to him into taking most of her belongings out of the overhead rack. He insisted that the stewardess force the gentleman in front to move his briefcase too, before he handed her a prepared list of foods he couldn't eat.

It was another of life's little ironies, the way the man across the aisle made himself ridiculous by trying so hard to look masterful.

He actually reminded Ben of Richard, superficially; deep voice, quick hands, large vocabulary. The difference was that Ben had seen Richard sit on a sweltering bus from Athens to Epidaurus, holding a Greek widow's two caged chickens and bag of feta cheese.

Poor Richard.

There was so much left that he'd wanted to do.

What does that mean? That God makes mistakes?

No. But it'll take me a while to get used to the empty place he's left behind.

I still think about the time Jessie told Richard he'd be more alive in a coma than the rest of us on our best days. He was paddling a canoe in a three-piece suit and reciting Shakespeare, with a baby robin he was raising asleep in his lap. It's hard to believe he can be reduced overnight to a name in an address book that has to be crossed off when I get home.

But that doesn't mean he wasn't difficult. He was a contrary, obviously, cryptic old Richard, *and* a contradiction. With his soft heart and his hard-bitten brain.

He was also a born teacher who'd already made himself exceptional, even before teaching took over his life.

Ben had seen it. He'd started out as Richard's student in Bloomington in 1940 — a quiet scholarship kid from Charlevoix, Michigan, with no conception of what college might be like.

And there was Richard — six-feet-five, red haired and wild with enthusiasm — running back and forth in front of a roomful of freshman English students, waving his arms when it got to be too much for him.

Ben asked himself where he would've been without Richard, while a stewardess blew up a life vest. Because Richard had taken him in hand. He'd dragged him to lectures and concerts, and invited him over to "debate the world's great issues" with his roommates and whoever else showed up. And it had changed the way Ben thought.

He smiled to himself, as he handed a Dramamine to the woman by the window, because he could still see the look of contempt on Richard's face when he'd told Richard he wanted to be a mining engineer or a forest ranger.

Richard had handed him his pack of Luckys and said, "Surely you're not serious!" with a pained expression bordering on disbelief. "The story of civilization is larger and deeper than a pond or a pit, Benjamin. And that's your proper quarry, pardon the pun. Not a stone quarry one blasts holes in while contemplating lunch! The development of thought! The revelations of God in human history! The accomplishments, and absurdities, and atrocities of man! That's the proper scope for a thinker like Benjamin Reese!"

And then, in the conscience-stricken, humble voice no one heard very often, Richard had had the audacity to add, "Of course, it's up to you. Far be it from me to try to pressure you in any way!"

Even back then Ben had been able to laugh, although he did tell him he was being presumptuous and infuriating. And Richard had looked shocked and hurt, which he was. He never could see how what he did looked to other people.

Which made Ben think about David Krause for the first time in years.

Krause was plenty smart and very perceptive about people. Sad he didn't do more when he was in school. And strange too, the violence he'd shown toward Richard. As though Richard had been the one who hadn't handed in the assignments.

But then we don't see ourselves clearly. We squint around the beams in our own eyes, and gloat over the moats in our neighbors'.

Of course, Richard had been right about

Ben's career. Because as Ben had become immersed in history and American studies, he stopped even asking what he might want to be, while he studied what he wanted to know.

Bill Taylor had had a lot to do with Ben's interest in history too. Bill had been doing graduate work on the Revolutionary War then, when he'd shared the apartment with Richard.

Ben looked out at the Heathrow tarmac as his plane revved for takeoff, and thought about the night he'd driven Bill to catch his train to boot camp.

He would've liked to talk to Bill again. To know what he would've done with himself and what he would've thought was important in 1960. But Bill had been shot down over France on his way back to the Channel, after one too many bombing runs across Germany.

The war changed everything for their whole generation. Which couldn't be more profoundly true, or more of an overworked sentiment.

Richard and Bill had enlisted early, in January of '42, less than a month after the attack on Pearl Harbor. Bill became a pilot, and Richard was trained as a military secretary, much to his disgust, though he was transferred to decoding and sent to Bletchley

Park before he'd been in a year.

Ben had waited to finish the semester before he enlisted. And he asked himself why, as his plane banked toward Ireland. The old WASP work ethic? Or a congenital fear of leaving anything undone?

He'd joined in February, a few days before he turned twenty, when Jim Cook, another of the history graduate students who'd shared Richard's rooms, had tried to enlist. But Jim had flat feet, and he'd ended up being classified 4F, which was still hard for him to accept.

Strange how things turn out. Ben never would've thought the three of them would end up at the same university.

And now that was finished too.

He leaned forward so he could see out the window as they flew over Ireland — which lay like a swatch of emerald velvet in an indigo sea — while he tried to imagine what life would be like without Richard.

Ben still couldn't think of him in the past tense. Even though he stared at the back of the seat in front of him and wished he'd done more for Richard when he'd had the chance. He should've gone to more concerts and restaurants and films when Richard asked. Because, contrary to the way it may have looked to the casual observer, it was harder for Richard to be alone than it was for Ben.

Death always made Ben wish he'd done more for the dead.

And it brought back Jessie's death. Like a wound that breaks open under a thin, fragile skin.

Still, he'd see him again. Eventually. And Richard was better off, Ben thought. Even though trying to imagine what Richard West would be like in heaven was an imponderable that would've made Ben laugh, if he hadn't been wondering who else he could talk to the way he'd talked to Richard.

CHAPTER THREE

Monday, November 21

Sally Poole was hardly awake as she climbed up the four floors of creaking wooden stairs and slumped into a one-armed desk — which is not to say that she wanted to be there. Attendance was required and she had no choice. She didn't much like French, and she didn't understand the literary verb forms as well as she had the conversational ones, and the teacher was either so disorganized or so brilliant she never explained anything so it made sense.

Actually, Miss Giardi was a strange lady in general. She was pathetic in an embarrassing sort of way. But it still gave you the creeps to listen to a fat woman in her fifties read love letters she'd gotten twenty-five years ago, from some small-time Italian writer. It didn't happen very often, but when it did, twenty midwestern freshmen tried to decide where to put their eyes.

She was known as "the Grazing Gazelle," which had to do with alliteration as well as the way she moved. It was something of an overblown bovine attempt at predatory grace, as though movement that was once seductive had passed into the realm of the unattainable, as fat and alcohol and inactivity had taken their usual percentage.

That particular day, Sally could see something was wrong as soon as Miss Giardi came through the door. She was plodding slowly toward her desk — her hair dirty and unkempt, her face fallen in upon itself, her silk dress clinging too closely to camouflage as much as the rest of the world might have liked.

"*Bonjour, mes élèves.* Ah, but that is a most unfortunate and bittersweet convention, *n'est pas?*, when one translates literally. For it is not a good day, it is a day of sorrow. You have heard the news, have you not?" Her eyes were red and swollen and circled with black mascara, and there were streaks in her powder as though she'd been crying for some time. "Dr. Richard West, the closest friend, yes, and the kindest of men. He has passed away, without warning, of a heart attack." She sat down heavily in her chair, and then she settled her double chin against her neck and exhaled unevenly. "There was no time to notify you ahead of class, but as you see, I am not able to continue. Not today." She seemed to be trying to keep her chin from trembling, and she raised her glasses

73

and wiped her eyes with a small rumpled square of embroidered linen. "We will meet this coming Wednesday as usual, so you must read again the De Maupassant. You will have to forgive me. I am overcome." She hurried out of the room with her handkerchief against her nose.

Sally looked at the guy next to her and shrugged her shoulders. "Who's Richard West?"

"Some English professor. I don't know him, myself."

"Well. I guess I'll go back and get some sleep. I don't have another class until four."

When she walked into the dorm, there was a message in her pigeonhole asking her to call Doug Smith, and she ran up three flights of stairs and threw her coat on her bed before shutting herself in the small graffiti-covered telephone booth next door to the freshman dorm counselor.

"Sally! Yeah, hi. I hope you're ready for this."

"What?"

"The old man? Friday night? The one who found us on the bench and took our names? He's the guy who just died. He had a heart attack right after we saw him."

"Oh no! Are you sure?"

"Yeah. The dean of men called me a while ago and he wants to talk to me after the funeral. The old guy wrote him a note about us, and it could've been the last thing he did."

"Are you kidding! You think we panicked him so much he croaked?"

"I don't know. He had to be pretty weird if that's all it took. Listen, I'll call you after I talk to him, OK?"

"Yeah. Thanks, Doug. I'll be here all afternoon."

The Presbyterian minister had known Richard well, and that always makes a difference in such ceremonies, especially if the minister believes what he's saying, which this one did.

Ben thought the French teacher was particularly sad, though, especially at the grave. He couldn't remember her name, but she'd once been the mistress of an Italian writer, and that one ragged fragment of a notorious past was expertly woven through most of her conversation.

Much to his own amazement and chagrin, Richard had attracted her attention, and he'd spent many of his off-hours trying not to hurt her feelings. He used to laugh and call it the "great theological crisis of my life, being pursued by Grace." That was it. Grace. Grace Giardi.

It was painful, watching her sob noisily and throw a faded rose on Richard's coffin, but it was also ludicrous. None of her behavior would have been peculiar if she'd been his wife. It was knowing how little there'd been between them that made it seem weird. To Ben, at least. Maybe nobody else was paying that much attention.

He watched the crowd and saw what he'd expected. The world is not populated by people who turn their backs on an opportunity to feel contempt.

Her short, puffy feet were hanging over her shoes and her make-up was running toward her quivering throat, while she swallowed strangling noises that reminded Ben of a small child.

She drifted away after the service was over, wandering alone in the middle of a crowd that looked the other way. And Ben felt sorry for her, without knowing what to say.

He talked to Richard's Aunt Gertrude (Richard's only living relative, who'd intended to die long before Richard did and gave the impression of being mildly put out) and arranged to drive her to her train.

Ben spoke with Richard's minister too, for

a few minutes, after she left.

And then he walked back to the grave, wondering why funeral directors think they have to hide the dirt under a blanket of artificial grass.

Richard had insisted on being buried in a plain pine box, which made tremendous sense to Ben. But the undertakers hadn't liked it, and now the cemetery people were sidling around the hole and glancing at Ben as though they'd appreciate it if he'd disappear.

"Afternoon, Ben."

"Hello, Chester. I was planning to drop by your office as soon as I finished here."

"Too bad about Richard." Chester Hansen was Hillsdale's chief of police, and had been for fifteen years. He'd attended the funeral in his perfectly creased tan uniform, and he was still holding his hat in his hands as though he didn't know what to do with it. "Did ya know he used to come in The Coffee Cup, three or four times a week?"

"No, I didn't."

"Yep. 'Bout five A.M., usually. He'd wake up and couldn't get back to sleep, and we'd shoot the breeze about all kinds of crazy stuff. He had a real way with words, Richard did. It was an education for me, just to listen to him."

"He showed me a world I'd never known existed. When I was just a kid, starting out in school." Ben reached down and picked up a clod of dirt that had escaped the artificial grass, and crushed it between his fingers, watching it scatter in the wind.

"I tell ya, Ben. Sitting there all alone like that. Fumbling around, trying to get his pills in his mouth. He was just a young man, really. Forty-three. Must've been horrible for him."

"I know." Ben didn't say anything else for a minute. He pushed his herringbone jacket back behind his elbows and put his hands in the pockets of his flannel pants. "So what time do you think he died?"

"Hold on just a minute." Chester reached inside his shirt pocket and adjusted the knobs that controlled his hearing aids. "Turned 'em down after the minister finished. Gets confusing in crowds when everybody's talkin'. You ask me when he died?"

Ben nodded as he watched two men roll up the fake grass, while another moved the casket-lowering machine in the direction of the white pine box.

"Body was found about nine Saturday morning. Coroner figured he'd been dead somewhere between six and twenty-four hours. Now, Ed Campbell was coming out of the English building Friday night when Richard was going in, and he says it was about eight, maybe a few minutes before. Says he looked normal. Nothing unusual about him that Ed could see. So all things being equal, he must've passed away between eight and three A.M."

"You think he was alone?"

"No sign of anybody else. Why?"

"I got a call from him right at nine —"

"Friday night?"

"Yeah. It was two in the morning in England, but he had them get me out of bed, and he told me he'd discovered 'an act of treachery that required retribution.' Just as he was about to explain that to me, somebody walked in and interrupted him. He hadn't gone home? He was still in his office?"

"Right. Now, a visitor, I s'pose that could make a difference."

"And it seems to me that whoever interrupted Richard probably had something to do with what prompted him to call. Otherwise I think he would've asked the person to wait outside, and finished talking to me. He actually made it sound more sinister than that, because what he said was, 'The culprit's just put in an appearance and I'll call you tomorrow.' "

"That's interesting." Chester rubbed the place on his nose where his glasses sat and looked past the fir trees toward the empty fields. "Gets more interesting the more you think about it too. So whoever it was, was in that office with him a few minutes after nine."

"I suppose you've still got it locked up?"

"Sure. You wanna take a look?"

"If it's OK with you. So who found him?"

"Nancy Shaffer. The department secretary. You knew Sarie quit?"

"No! When was that?"

"Three weeks ago maybe. Must've been right after you left on sabbatical."

"Any idea why?"

"Can't say I've looked into it. One thing I felt kinda bad about though."

"What's that?"

"That apprentice of yours? She was waiting outside in the hall there, when we were taking the body out. Said she had an appointment with him for nine forty-five."

"She sent me the telegram, but I haven't talked to her. I saw her at the service though, in the back. Have you got plans, or can we stop over at his office?"

"Now's as good a time as any. Let me get my car and I'll meet you over there."

They climbed the old wooden stairs to the

second floor and turned right toward Richard's office. The English department was officially closed because of the funeral, and no one else seemed to be in. A young man passed them in the hall, coming from the direction they were headed, and Ben thought he looked familiar. Of course, it might have been more significant if he hadn't. Ben had been working with students so long, most of them looked familiar.

Richard's office smelled like books. They filled the walls and lay in stacks on the floor. There were many other artifacts too (which is the way Ben tended to think of objects, as an archivist), and each piece made a comment about Richard's character. It was organized along unorthodox lines, but there was a sense of order imposed upon all of it: the rocks and the coral, the collection of walking sticks, the ostrich egg, the goat skull, the three mortar and pestles, and the elephant-foot wastepaper basket Richard had inherited from an uncle. He never could stand to use it, and yet he couldn't bring himself to give it away, so it stood in a corner beside a radiator with a book press sitting on top.

There were plants on the window sills, and three piles of paper on the huge desk (an American oak desk with round brass knobs, circa 1885). The blotter was pushed forward and slanted toward the right, if you were sitting at the desk like Ben was. And it looked to him as though Richard had slumped across it, with his head lying on the left.

"Yep. Face down, arms bent on either side of his head, right hand under his throat. Five nitroglycerin pills were scattered across the desk, and the lid was off, and the bottle was overturned like you'd expect. Phone was off the hook too. Like he'd tried to call for help and couldn't make it."

"Did you fingerprint?"

"Nope. Looked like natural causes to the coroner. I thought so too, of course, or I would've taken it further. This phone call, though, it makes you wonder if it's not more complicated. Autopsy report said natural causes."

"You mind if I look around a while?"

"No. Go ahead. Here, you take his keys. I'll get a cup of coffee and head over to the office. Might give the coroner a buzz too. Just bring 'em over when you're done." Chester smoothed his thick gray hair and slid his visored cap into place, adjusting it carefully out of habit. But he didn't leave right away. He stood and studied Ben, with his thumbs hooked inside his belt. "I suppose you intelligence boys must've been trained to be pretty observant."

"I was mostly involved in materials evaluation."

"You scouted though, didn't you?"

"Yeah."

"Richard said you did a lotta reconnaissance. Never saw combat myself. Too old, I guess. Got stuck as an M.P. Always wondered what it wouldda been like. Matter of fact, I've kinda looked for you at the V.F.W."

Ben glanced at Chester's calm, uncomplicated face, but he didn't say anything.

"Thought maybe you'd want to come with me sometime. We sit around and chew the fat and it's kinda interesting, hearing what other people did in the war."

"Thanks, Chester. Maybe sometime. I guess I don't dwell on the war as much as some people do."

"There some special reason for that?"

"It's not that I regret having gone. But I don't want to hear somebody tell me about something they didn't do. You know what I mean? Stories can get embroidered after a while."

"Yeah, that's true. Sure. Anyway, maybe I oughtta send the boys back in here when we get a breather, and let 'em see what they can find."

"Good. I'll bring the keys over as soon as I'm done."

"You know, you might want to talk to Ed Campbell again. I couldn't get much out of him, if you know what I mean, and you might stand a better chance, being a professor and all."

"Yeah, maybe I will. Thanks, Chester. I'll try not to leave any prints."

Ben sat in Richard's chair and stared at the desk. He leaned over after a minute, and turned his head so he could see the surface without reflections.

He examined the edge next, and found a rough spot above the center drawer. He pulled out the small magnifying glass his father had made into a key ring for him, for the close work he did every day, and slipped it out of its leather cover.

There were five dark blue fibers, probably wool, caught in a nick above the drawer. They might have come from a sweater, but he doubted it. The ends had been cut. And the fibers were stiffer. Straighter. More like a tuft from some kind of carpet.

The color was wrong for the one on the floor. But there was a pillow, on the old wicker guest chair, that was made from a blue Chinese rug.

The fibers matched, when Ben compared them. And he told himself to remember to tell Chester, so he could ask his lab people to collect them, whenever they came back in.

He glanced through the papers on Richard's desk, and the stack of unopened mail. And then he pulled a handkerchief out of his pocket and used it to examine the electric typewriter on the metal stand on his left. He unlocked the center drawer with it too, and laid the pocket calendar on the desk, before sliding Richard's address book into the inside pocket of his jacket.

Bernard Greene's personnel file was the only folder in that drawer, and Ben read through it, taking notes on a memo pad. He swiveled around to the horizontal files and made a cursory inspection of those; then he turned back to the desk and began with the drawers on the right, underneath Richard's phone.

There wasn't anything of particular interest in the first two, but he found a locked walnut writing box shoved toward the back of the bottom drawer.

It was an English lap desk, and the small brass key on Richard's ring turned easily in the lock. The interior was covered with black leather, and there were places for pen and ink, and a large sloping surface meant for writing, which also served as a lid for two storage compartments underneath.

Ben opened the one closest to him and found a photograph of a woman in a British nurse's uniform with "Yours always, Glenna," written on the bottom across one of her hands. Directly under it, folded inside a woman's linen handkerchief, was a man's wedding band. And underneath that was a British marriage license, as well as the corresponding American military forms.

The divorce papers were on the bottom, naming Glenna Phillips West as the guilty party, by reason of adultery and desertion.

Ben held the papers and the ring and the photograph in his lap and looked out the window past a wilted fern, thinking that might explain a lot of things. Except why he hadn't talked about it. Why wouldn't Richard let anybody in?

He'd known Richard had been involved with someone in England during the war, but he'd never discussed it in any detail. And Ben had watched the walls go up for fifteen years. At least that's the way it had looked to him. The layers of fat and the manner of an Oxford don, designed to discourage advances and keep Richard from being hurt.

Ben watched the sun slice through the window and followed a few last leaves blown from the trees. And then he carefully laid what was left of Richard's marriage back in the antique box.

He tilted the worn leather chair back and sat still for several moments with his hands behind his head. His eyes were hot and tired, and he opened his mouth as wide as he could and rubbed the joints on either side of his jaw. Then he purposefully scanned the length of each bookshelf, from one end, book by book, to the other, pausing longest on the shelf full of Richard's works of criticism and literary biography.

He shifted his jaw to the left and tapped his eyeteeth together, then looked through Richard's appointment calendar, concentrating on his last day.

Friday, Nov. 18. — 9:00 — Chaucer. 10:00 — graduate tutorial, Blake. 11:00 — Intro. to Poetry. 12:15 — Rotary.

"Columbus" was written across the whole afternoon. Maybe that was something. And he'd have to ask Nancy. Did she handle Richard's personal correspondence? I bet he did his own. But where did he keep his copies, if that were true? And what were his normal procedures? When did he stop by his office most days and pick up his mail, for instance? And who were his graduate assistants? Assuming he had any. Richard was a teacher who liked to teach.

It was hard to know where to look, when you didn't know what you were after. Anything could be important. He'd have to fit himself into Richard's life, the day-in and day-out routine of it, so he could see what stood out as unusual. Assuming that anything did.

If he wasn't alone and there had been a confrontation, and this wasn't simply an attack of angina, Richard's last moments on earth must have been filled with anger and hatred and fear. Worse than the war, in some ways. There's an impersonality to combat that makes it less vicious than murder. But then, Richard had never been in battle, and that might have made it harder too.

Murder. That was an interesting choice of words.

Yes, but where had it come from?

Not from the evidence. There isn't any.

All I've got is the sound of Richard's voice reverberating in my head, saying, "I've discovered an act of treachery that deserves retribution . . . and the culprit's just put in an appearance."

Ben stood up, with his coat behind his elbows and his hands in his pants pockets, and began walking back and forth, studying the floorboards and the threadbare oriental.

He pulled the empty wastepaper basket out from under the desk and found a scrap of brown wrapping paper on the floor behind it. He picked it up and put it in his wallet.

And then he tried to remember where he'd stuck the set of keys Richard had given him years ago, when he and Jessie were living on Poe Road, and Richard had just moved from Ann Arbor.

Ben had finished examining the mailboxes (the pigeonholes that belonged to the English department, as well as administration) and he'd just started down the stairs, when he heard typing in the small office in the alcove next to Nancy Shaffer's door. Ben knew it was one of the graduate student offices, and if it was Campbell's, Ben decided to see if they could talk then, before he got battered by jet lag again.

"Edward Campbell" was written in very small, unattractive blue ballpoint letters on a stained index card thumbtacked to the door frame, and Ben knocked on the door and waited.

The typing stopped but nothing else happened, so Ben knocked softly again in the cool afternoon silence of the empty halls.

Someone was walking toward the door,

but he paused on the other side, and said "Yes?" in a hesitant voice.

"Mr. Campbell?"

The door opened three or four inches, and a long, thin face Ben had seen at the funeral squinted around the peeling paint.

"I'm Ben Reese. I was a friend of Richard West's, and I wonder if I could talk to you for a minute."

"Now?" The eye Ben could see looked anxious and the door didn't open any further.

"If you wouldn't mind. It won't take long."

Edward Campbell looked at his typewriter first, but he went ahead and opened the door. And then he stood behind it as Ben stepped into an office the size of a broom closet where an explosion of papers and books appeared to have taken place. There was a small institutional wooden desk with a portable typewriter on it jammed in a corner, and there was one battered desk chair that flipped backward dangerously when Ed closed the door and sat down in it.

He had no choice but to sit while Ben stood. There wasn't room for two people to stand, any more than there was room for another chair.

"Dr. West was very interested in your

work on Samuel Johnson."

Ed Campbell didn't say anything. He just blushed and blinked uncontrollably with his whole face, while he wrapped his arms around his ribs.

"But the reason I'm here is that Chester Hansen told me you saw Dr. West the night he died."

Campbell nodded, then reached into the pile of paper clips on his desk and began sliding two of them together.

"He said you told him you saw Richard about eight."

"It might've been a few minutes before." Edward Campbell whispered it and kept his eyes on his paper clips.

"How much before, do you think?"

"It couldn't have been earlier than ten of eight. And I guess it might have been as late as five minutes after."

"How did Richard look?"

"Fine. Just like he always did."

"Was he worried or upset?"

"No, he was whistling, and he seemed kind of amused. Like he was thinking about something he thought was funny." Ed glanced at Ben quickly and then looked back at his own hands.

"Was he carrying anything?"

"His briefcase. And his pipe, I think." It

was an even quieter whisper.

And Ben had to concentrate to hear him. "His thin briefcase that looks like an envelope, or his thick one?"

"His thin one."

"He wasn't carrying anything else?"

Ed shook his head without turning in Ben's direction.

"And that was all you saw of him?"

Edward Campbell had finished stringing all his paper clips together, and he started taking them apart again as he nodded. It was hot in that office, and he was wearing a short-sleeved shirt, and he was so thin, his wrists and his elbow bones seemed larger than the arms in between.

Ben watched him for a minute without saying anything; and then he asked if he'd seen anyone else in the building.

"Not right then." Ed picked up his stapler, a chrome one with a round, flat dome on the top. "But I did later."

"Who?"

"I don't know. I forgot my briefcase, and I had to come back for it. While I was in here, I heard someone in high heels walking down the hall." Ed looked away again, and pulled the metal catch out of the back of the stapler.

"Did you tell Chester Hansen?"

Campbell shook his head.

"Why not?"

"He didn't ask."

"Do you know who it was?"

"No."

"I see." Ben was trying to watch him without seeming to, without making him more nervous. And he glanced casually from time to time at his unassuming bony face with its residual teenage acne, at the self-conscious body pulled in on itself, at the arms and legs that looked as though they'd never left a desk, and the pale blue eyes that squinted and blinked relentlessly every four or five seconds.

"What time was it when you heard her?"

"I'd say between eight-thirty and nine."

"Was there anyone else you saw or heard?"

"Yes." He whispered it again as he played with the spring in his stapler. "Someone must have been washing the floors. There was a sign downstairs that said 'wet floor.' And there was somebody typing up here."

"Do you know who it was?"

"No." The spring broke in his hand; it slid out the back of the stapler and unwound in a hopeless curve.

"You're sure?"

"I wasn't paying attention. I have to defend my dissertation week after next and it's not done! It's not done competently anyhow, and I have no reason to think that it ever will be."

"I remember what that feels like. Only too well, unfortunately."

Ed Campbell looked even more anxious and laid the stapler on the desk very carefully.

"But you'll live through it. Everybody does."

"Everybody doesn't. Some people fall by the wayside." Ed smiled hopelessly, and when he swallowed, his Adam's apple shifted so far it almost looked painful.

"I know Dr. West thought highly of both your writing and your research, and he wasn't easy to please."

"He was the only professor in the English department I could talk to."

"But now he's gone. So that's got to be hard on you."

Ed didn't say anything.

Ben looked past him at a shelf of books on Samuel Johnson. "So that's all you can remember about Friday night?"

Ed nodded again and slid his hands between his knees.

"Are you teaching this semester?"

"Yes, I am." He licked his lips as though

his mouth was dry.

Ben tried to imagine him in front of a room full of kids, and failed. "Thanks for talking to me. You've helped a lot and I appreciate it."

"Didn't Dr. West die of a heart attack?"

"Yeah, he did, but I was a good friend of his, and I was out of the country, and I guess I'm just interested in what he went through."

"I'll have to replace him on my dissertation committee." Edward Campbell looked even more panicked than he had before.

Ben tried to think of something to say that might make it easier, and all he came up with was, "I don't know that there's anything I can do, but if I can help, or you want to talk, give me a call. You can leave a message at my office, or call me at home, either one."

Edward Campbell didn't answer him directly. But he smiled self-consciously as Ben closed the door.

There was a huge painting above Ben's bed, done wet and loose like a study of Frankenthaler. But there wasn't much furniture for a room that size. Just a rocking chair by the fireplace, a television in a bookcase opposite the bed, and a plain maple desk that had once been a kitchen table, back by the door to the bathroom.

The big bed sat right on the plank floor next to a black and white calfskin rug, with a carpenter's trunk set against the wall that Ben used as a bedside table.

There were four tall narrow windows, and high walls with carved moldings, and there was a sense of peace and space and quiet which had settled on that bedroom like a comforter smoothed across old sheets.

But Ben woke up sweating in the big white room, rolled up in his sheets like a moth in a cocoon, with his head underneath a pillow. He threw it off the way a diver comes up for air, and then he turned on the bedside light and propped himself up on his elbows.

He was breathing like he'd been running, and he watched the corners as though shadows can't be trusted. He'd gotten over expecting Jessie to be there, but he hadn't exactly adjusted. He'd just learned not to close his eyes until he'd been awake long enough to feel safe.

He turned the light off after a while and got out of bed. The sky was overcast and cold and the room was dark. He walked to the window and stood there sweating, watching the heavy gray sky.

He went into the bathroom and splashed cold water on his face, and when he came back, he opened the drawer of Jessie's desk.

The Camels were there with the ash tray and the matches, and he sat down in the dark in the chair by the desk and tapped the end of a cigarette against a thumb nail. He inhaled and it made him dizzy a few seconds later. He only smoked cigarettes after one of his dreams. It was like a temporary reprieve. Or a reward for having lived to dream about it. Except that he considered it a gift, being alive to relive the blood bath.

At least that night, it wasn't Omaha Beach. Though Ben hadn't gone in with the first wave of assault troops. The invasion he was a part of very few people knew about. He landed the night before, June 5th, 1944, attached by Intelligence to the First Battalion Canadian Strike Force D2.

There were a hundred and five of them (thirty-five in each sub), and they'd gone in after dark in inflatable rafts to take out the big guns that shelled them from fortified bunkers on the cliffs above the sea.

Casualties were pretty much what they'd expected — ninety-five percent. And they got the survivors out with the hospital evacuation ships forty-eight hours after the invasion.

But seventy percent of the men who went in were left dead on the cliffs and the beaches. Which might seem like an ordinary statistic, unless you've seen it with your own eyes.

Ben wasn't badly hurt. Just shrapnel in various parts of his body.

Not like later, after scouting across France and Belgium. Going in first, night after night. Usually with one or two other guys, sometimes three at the most. Capturing German command posts. Photographing their maps and papers. Trying to figure out where they were heading, and how many there were, and what kind of equipment they had. Trying to help the underground too, learn how to forge their documents.

The rest of the men called them "The Nighttime Special," even before the Malmédy Massacre, when they were the ones who found the bodies. Hundreds of dead captured Americans under a powdering of dirt and snow, slaughtered by the Germans as they moved out.

Finding those bodies did something to the GIs, and the next battle was savage and lasted three days.

But he had made it.

Through France. Through Belgium. Through The Battle of the Bulge in the Ardennes Forest. Down through Luxembourg, to the Saarbrucken Forest across the German border near Trier.

That's what he'd dreamt about. Getting careless. Asking a ninety-day kid lieutenant who didn't know anything, how it looked in front. He should've asked what G-2 said was out there, but he didn't, and the kid didn't understand.

So he had walked out in three feet of snow in a khaki uniform after a dawn raid and got pinned down by machine-gun fire.

Gene was killed before Ben stopped the machine gun. And then two Tiger tanks came out of nowhere, running straight at him. He took out one of the tanks with Gene's bazooka, but the other one put fifteen thirty-caliber slugs (7.62 mm, to be precise) inside his own skin.

He lay there for three hours, between the lines during a firefight, bleeding to death and packing his wounds with snow. Later, they said the snow's what saved him.

And yet Ben had looked down on his own dead body that morning, lying on a white drift. He'd seen the future, already happening. But the next instant he'd known — with the same certainty that he knew his own name — that it wouldn't happen. He'd known he was about to be saved. In order to do something for somebody, sometime.

If he talked about it out loud while he

smoked his Camel, it made it go away faster and seem less real. He never dreamed about it in perfect detail anyway. He dreamt parts that were real, and some things that were worse.

The worst one happened a couple months after Jessie died, when he was already lost inside and didn't want to come back. In that dream he was moving into an empty town, at night, alone with Tommy, some place in Belgium, probably near Malmédy. The Germans were supposed to have moved out, and there was no smoke and no sound and no sign of life. But you knew there were eyes behind the walls. You could feel bodies breathing, watching you walk, waiting to take you in the back.

And then you hear a door open behind you, slow and soft and sinister, and you can feel a finger move against metal and you turn around to defend your back — and blow your best friend's face off.

But the end of every dream was always the same, the real ending, after the tanks by Trier. He never could make himself wake up until he'd been strapped on a stretcher and lashed to the undercarriage of a Piper Cub, the artillery spotter that flew him into France to the railhead.

They'd expected him to die on the way,

but they'd sent him out. They gave him another chance and he made it. He'd flown through treetops, under the antiaircraft guns, so cold it made him cry, until they landed and the impact knocked him out. He never made it to the train that took him into Paris, not in the dream. He always woke in the cold, in the air, flying through the treetops, screaming.

CHAPTER FOUR

Tuesday, November 22

"Did you see him the day he died?"

"Briefly. On his way out the door." Nancy Shaffer pushed her black leather headband farther back on her head and squinted across the English department office toward the water cooler. "He had two classes that morning, and his Blake tutorial."

"Do you remember the name of the graduate student?"

"Frank Marquez."

"Did they meet in Richard's office?"

"Not Friday. They went to Dr. West's house. He'd made doughnuts, or coffee cake or something. You know how he liked to bake."

"So you didn't actually talk to Dr. West?"

"I just said hello to him a few minutes before eight. He had that lunch meeting later, and then he was driving to Columbus."

"Why?"

"I know he was planning to visit the University Museum. Maybe it's the Anthropology Museum. The one where they have the mound-builder displays? One of the anthropology professors is a friend of his."

"Ah. Waldo Hubbard."

"That sounds right."

Ben had only met him once, but he was an old friend of Richard's, and he was struggling through the last stages of Parkinson's disease. "Was Richard planning to go anywhere else?"

"He didn't mention anything. I know he often went to the zoo. Of course I don't know if he meant it, you know how he joked with a straight face, but I remember one time he said he was teaching a parrot to say Ludwig von Beethoven."

"Yeah, he probably was."

"Friday he just said he wouldn't be back in the office before I left for the day, so he'd leave me a note for Monday, if there was anything special he wanted done first thing."

"Didn't he have office hours on Monday?"

"Ten to twelve. But I get in at eight, while he's teaching, and if he leaves me a note, I can get started."

"You do all the department work?"

"He was planning to hire someone part-time. Now that I've moved into Sarie's job."

"I was surprised to hear she'd left."

"It was a surprise to everybody." Nancy dropped a pen in her center drawer with a carefully neutral expression.

And yet it looked to Ben like she was trying not to say something more. "So why do you think she quit?"

"You want my honest opinion? Or you want me to be discreet?"

"I'd like to hear what you really think."

"I think she was too wishy-washy to work for Dr. West." Nancy's broad hands had gripped the edge of her desk, and she was watching her thumbs slide back and forth. "You know what he was like, he'd toss instructions at you over his shoulder as he ran out the door. Sarie couldn't take it in that fast. My father was a lot like Dr. West, so it didn't bother me that much. I'd holler at him and drag him back if I didn't understand what he meant, and then he'd apologize for not explaining. There's nobody in the department who can replace him. And I hope they don't make a big mistake."

"But Sarie never talked to you about it?"

"Not directly." Nancy bent her large, gray-haired head and began lining up the edges of the papers on her desk, making neat symmetrical piles with equal distances between them. "To tell you the truth, I think they drove each other crazy. She was slow and disorganized, and that was frustrating for him because he did everything so fast."

Nancy smiled and shook her head and her face lost the tight, set lines. "He'd say things like, 'Get me that guy Smith on the phone!' And I'd say, 'Wait a minute, which Smith?' I thought it was kind of funny, myself, but Sarie would just sit there and stare at her hands."

"Does she still take care of her father?"

"I think it's her uncle. He's an invalid, but I don't know what's wrong with him."

"It's good of her, to do that." Ben picked a piece of lint off his corduroy pants and laid his right ankle on his left thigh, before looking to see how Nancy reacted.

"Oh, I know, she's a nice person. But there was a definite personality clash."

"Did Richard pick up his mail Friday?"

"He must have. There were several things in his mailbox, and they were gone Saturday morning."

"You remember anything in particular?"

"Nothing special. One or two political letters. He was always writing senators and congressmen and the chairman of the Foreign Relations Committee."

"And wondering why nobody else did. Did he type his personal correspondence?"

"He was very particular about that. I did everything that was related to the university, but he used the typewriter he bought for his personal correspondence, as well as the early drafts of his literary articles and political essays."

"Did he keep copies of his own letters?"

"He was careless about that, in my opinion. He made carbons of his political letters, and his financial correspondence, but other than that, he never bothered."

"What time is the mail delivered?"

"Early afternoon. I get it in the boxes by two usually."

"It was still in his pigeonhole when you went home at four?"

"I think so." Nancy adjusted the cuffs of her suit coat, while gazing at a cactus on a filing cabinet as though she were trying to visualize Richard's mailbox. "I mean, I didn't notice, especially. But he hadn't come in."

Ben had already gotten up and walked to the window, where he picked up the cord to the old venetian blinds and gazed across campus toward The Coffee Cup. "Do you remember if he'd gotten a package?"

"Seems like he did. I do everybody's mail at once and I can't say I recall for sure, but someone got a package, something I had to work to fit in the box."

"Do you usually come in on Saturday?"

"If there's anything pressing. My husband went hunting, and I just thought I'd come in and clean up a few odds and ends. I'm glad I did. I wouldn't like to think of Dr. West lying there all weekend."

"But finding him must have been a shock. You have a key to his office?"

"I gave it to the police. The door was unlocked, though. And now that I think about it, the janitor would've found him when he came in to clean. I nursed during the war, so that stood me in good stead. You know what I mean. When I opened the door."

"Ben! Ben, over here! Sorry I didn't get to talk to you after the funeral, but I had an alumni meeting." President James Cook smoothed his tie with a practiced hand and the gold ring on his little finger flashed for a second in the sun. "I saw the long arm of the law walking your way, and I couldn't wait."

"How are you, Jim? How's Mary Ann?"

"She's fine. She's taken the children to Florida to visit her family for ten days, but she'll be back Sunday. Her father's not very well, and she felt she ought to go. You haven't seen the kids in a while, have you? We just got their school pictures back this week." Jim pulled his wallet out of the breastpocket of his suit coat and handed Ben two small color prints.

"Boy, they're growing up. How old are they now?"

"James is nine, and Sarah's seven."

"They're both very good-looking."

"They are, aren't they? They must have inherited it from their mother." Jim looked at the snapshots for a second himself, and then put them back in his wallet. "I feel terrible about Richard."

"I know. I do too."

"It's such a shame, Ben. Why did he have to be his own worst enemy? I remember when he was as skinny as a rail. Remember, back in Bloomington? He looked like a starving Swedish farmer, instead of a doctor's son from the best side of Chicago."

"I suppose it would've helped if he'd lost thirty pounds, but he inherited the heart condition. His father was thin, and he died when he was forty-five."

"Did he? I guess I'd forgotten that. Of course, Richard didn't talk to me about personal matters the way he did you. I don't think he ever felt the same about me after he got back from the war." Jim moved his smooth, narrow briefcase from one hand to the other, and looked past Ben toward the grove of trees outside the administration offices. "To tell you the truth, I don't think he ever forgave me for being 4F."

"He *never* felt that way!"

"You're sure?"

"Absolutely. Richard didn't blame you for what you couldn't help. We were all just different after the war. We enlisted as kids and we came back old men. Of course I was much younger than the two of you!"

"Don't rub it in! By what, five or six years maybe?"

"Yeah. But seriously, he never held it against you."

"I do think there was a feeling of strain between us. Not always. But sometimes."

"You disagreed on several fundamental principles of education. Tenure. Budget priorities. Graduate tutorials. With you being president and him the head of the English department, how could there not be conflict?"

"Perhaps. I hadn't thought of it in quite those terms. But what a great character he was! There'll never be another like Richard West. He really had a remarkable mind, Ben. Even if I did take exception to his opinions from time to time. And as I'm sure you know, his passing is a real blow for the English department, and it'll take a while to repair the damage. So when are you leaving for England?"

"I don't know. I'll postpone it until after the first of the year anyway. I accomplished quite a bit while I was there, and several things have come up here I ought to take care of. Listen, I hate to rush, but I'm on my way to see Chester."

"Why? I can't imagine that you find him stimulating."

"I like Chester. And he's letting me go over his paperwork."

"I apologize, Ben. I didn't mean that to sound so condescending. But why would you want to? You don't think Richard's death was suspicious, do you?"

"No. Although there are 'one or two rather suggestive points.' "

"Quoting Conan Doyle are we? Holmes would've been utterly bored by this death! Richard had a heart condition. It could've happened any time."

"That's true. But I have to stay here anyway; I'm the executor of his will. And I suppose it makes me feel better, following his footsteps those last few days."

"There's no doubt that he died of a heart attack?"

"No, none at all."

"That's what everyone assumed, but the obituary was kind of vague. You know how they are."

"I miss him, Jim. I haven't had a hot discussion since he drove me to the airport."

"Then drop over sometime! I mean it. Let's have a drink together, or go out to eat. Of course, we'll have to plan ahead. You can imagine what my schedule's like."

"That's why they pay presidents more than archivists. I'll see you later, Jim. Give my regards to Mary Ann."

They smiled at each other, then turned away. James Cook walked toward the president's office, swinging his Italian briefcase and tucking his paisley scarf inside the neck of his cashmere overcoat. Ben trotted across campus, shuffling though the leaves in his desert boots, wondering when Richard's office was last cleaned.

Ellen Winter opened the door of the small conference room where she worked and stepped into Ben Reese's office without looking up from her journal. She was on her way to the drinking fountain, and she jumped before she could stop herself, when she realized there was a man she'd never seen before sitting in Dr. Reese's chair.

He seemed to be staring at the center drawer, but then his head snapped up and it looked as though he'd started to leap up but changed his mind.

"Hey, lady! You took my breath away!"

"I'm sorry. I didn't see you either."

A small piece of tobacco was stuck at one corner of his mouth, and he picked it off while he recovered himself, and then smiled at Ellen. "Yeah, well, I just stopped in to talk to Dr. Reese. I made a phone call too I should've made yesterday, while I was waiting for him to get back. So who are you?"

"Ellen Winter." He looked about thirty, and he had dark eyes and a strong jaw, and Ellen thought he was very good-looking when he smiled. The hardness disappeared, and his eyes seemed more straightforward. "Do you know Janie, his secretary? She can probably tell you when he'll be in."

"I tried. She's out to lunch. But it's no big deal, I'll catch him later. Can I drop you somewhere?"

He'd already stood up, and although he wasn't very large or very powerful-looking, there was something about him that forced Ellen to notice him physically. She found herself measuring his shoulders and the shape of his thighs. And she didn't like the fact that he could make her do that. "I don't think so. But thank you anyway. I've got work to do here."

Neither Frank Marquez (the graduate student Richard had met with before he drove to Columbus), nor Waldo Hubbard at Ohio

State had much to add when Ben phoned. Their conversations with Richard on the day he died had been just what they always were. He hadn't seemed preoccupied or upset. He hadn't told them what his plans were for the rest of the day. And both of them said they missed arguing with him already.

Ben had hung up the phone and was looking out the window of his small, businesslike office, thinking how much worse Waldo sounded.

I probably ought to go visit him, now that Richard's gone. They don't have kids and his wife doesn't drive —

"Dr. Reese? Am I interrupting?"

"Ellen! No, come on in. How are you?"

"Fine. I'm sorry about Dr. West."

"Thank you for sending the telegram."

"Oh, you're welcome. I called Maggie, but she wasn't home. I wish there was something more I could've done."

Ben looked at her and wondered whether that reply was a matter of convention or actual conviction, and then decided to change the subject. Ellen seemed older than most of his students, and that sometimes made it difficult to know where to draw the lines. "You sent the Aubusson wall hanging?"

"To the Brooklyn Museum of Fine Arts, insured for fifteen hundred dollars."

"And what about the journals?"

"I've been working through *Classical Studies*, and *Art Bulletin for Restoration*, but I haven't touched *Coin World International*."

"That's OK. You've made a good start. And now I think it's time you got your hands dirty."

"What does that mean?"

"We will begin with the field of numismatics."

"About which I know nothing!"

"That doesn't matter. I have a little surprise for you in the catacombs." He smiled and stood up, and then checked his coat pockets to make sure he had his keys.

They talked about films down three flights of stairs into the basement of the library, which did give the impression of being a labyrinthine crypt. Cool, dark, silent except for the hum of the furnaces and the air blowers. There were no marble floors and carved arches like there were on the upper floors, and no painted marbleized friezes — just concrete blocks and wire partitions with locked gates protecting aisle after aisle of shelves and drawers.

"I think I put them in here." Ben opened a wooden drawer in the middle of an aisle, and began sorting through small glass-topped boxes and leather bags. "I found them last summer in a drawer of butterflies in the old science museum. Go ahead and look around. It's interesting, isn't it? I'm still amazed by what turns up."

"Are these things valuable?" Ellen's eyes swept the rows of busts and statuary and then turned toward the shelves of oversized fossils.

"Not those particularly, but there're a lot of things here that are. The alumni have donated whole collections of coins and paintings and rare books. Usually because they remember what it was like for them, and they want students here, kids from small podunk midwestern towns like they were, to be able to appreciate them too."

"That's a nice thing to do. When they could've sold them, or let their families have them."

"Of course, you have to remember that all artifacts are pieces of history even if they aren't valuable. What we tend to think of as 'History,' is basically the subjective interpretation of public acts, usually written from a considerable distance. Created objects are bits of real people's lives, and the day-to-day culture in which they lived. And I like that, for some reason. Ah, here they are. Finally. I was beginning to think they'd disappeared." Ben handed her a small, stained cardboard box.

Ellen took the lid off and carefully removed a layer of cotton, uncovering four crude, half-spherical copper coins which managed to give the impression of great age.

"They still have to be identified and dated, and I thought it would be an interesting project. Now what's the first thing you'd do?"

"Look through the reference books?"

"Right. But what if you don't find them there?"

"Photograph them, I guess, and send the slides to whatever museums specialize in ancient coins."

"Good. I'd try the British National Museum, or the Berlin Museum maybe, or even the Vienna Numismatics Museum. And since you'll be working in the conference room, I'll keep them upstairs, in the safe in my office. I'll be around a few more weeks, so if you run into a snag, I can give you names of people who might be able to save you time."

"You aren't going back to England right away?"

"I have to settle Dr. West's affairs first." Ben followed her through the narrow hall and watched her bent head as she rubbed the coins between her fingers as though the feel of them was good against her skin. "So what made you want to become an apprentice?"

"Well, I'm a humanities major, but I want to be a writer. And I'm trying to learn all kinds of other things so I have something to talk about when the time comes."

"That's what I would've done."

"And when I met you, when I was doing that paper on Branwell Brontë? It seemed to me that what you do must be great experience for a writer. Of course, my mother got me interested in historical things before that. She has an antique business that deals in small English pieces.

"I used to watch her with her barometers, and her pen and ink stands, and it was almost like they'd had lives of their own, and she could tell stories about them. That's what I did as a little kid. I'd go to the shop with her, and put paper in her typewriter, and use candlesticks and hourglasses as ideas for stories, the way someone else might use a murder weapon."

"I was raised in northern Michigan, and I called the hunting dogs when I was a kid and went to the woods." Ben grabbed a handful of cashews from the jar on Janie's desk and opened his door for Ellen. "So what's your father do? I'm sorry, that's none of my business."

"I don't mind. He's a judge."

"Ah. My dad's a tool-and-die maker. He's an inventor really, in his own way. Let me get those in the safe." Ben turned to the cabinet on the left of his desk and went through the combination, swinging the heavy metal door open on creaking hinges.

"So how was it that you and Dr. West and President Cook all ended up at a private university like Alderton?"

"My wife and I were teaching here, and Dr. West came to visit. He was working at the University of Michigan, and he liked the smallness of Alderton, the way you can really get to know your students and work with them individually. And then three years ago, when President Morrison retired, Dr. Cook applied for the position."

"So does that make you feel closer to President Cook than you would otherwise, having known him a long time?"

"Sure. I think so. We don't see each other socially a whole lot because we're both too busy, but yes. He and I even went down to enlist together during the war. Anyway, leave a message with Janie if I can help in the next few weeks. And when you need the coins, I can give them to her, if I know ahead of time."

"Could I make an appointment to interview you, like we talked about before? Especially now that Dr. —"

"Sure. How 'bout next week? After Thanksgiving vacation?"

"Fine. I'll arrange it with Janie. Did that man find you?"

"What man?"

"I came out of the conference room about an hour and a half ago, and Janie was out to lunch, and someone was sitting at your desk. He said he was using your phone while he waited for you to get back."

"What did he look like?"

"He wasn't very old. He could've been a professor, or he could've been a graduate student. He had dark hair and he was good-looking, but his clothes were rumpled and kind of dirty. I did notice one thing, though. He was wearing leather gloves, and I thought that was odd, if he was using your phone like he said."

"That's interesting. Yeah, I'm glad you mentioned it. Thanks."

Ben slid the key into Richard's lock and opened his kitchen door. Something smelled funny already; probably the cheese on the counter under the glass dome. He'd come back later and clean out the refrigerator and the cupboards, and maybe Maggie would come too and help salvage whatever was still good.

Richard had more kitchen equipment than Ben could believe possible, having specialized in French, Greek, and Chinese cuisine. And it took Ben a while to look through it.

He walked into the bedroom next, without noticing anything unusual. There was a double bed with a blue-striped Greek spread, a chest of drawers, a closet door with nothing behind it of particular interest, a disreputable Chesterfield chair and footstool, the two infamous brass floor lamps from the Salvation Army, and the Russian icon of the crucifixion Richard had bought in England during the war — which, aside from its artistic and religious value, was now worth an incredible amount of money.

The bathroom was what Ben had expected. Everything was put away, the same way it was in the bedroom and the kitchen. There were clean towels, shabby but still serviceable, and old nondescript fixtures. There were no sleeping pills, and no medications in the cabinet except nitroglycerin, aspirin, and Alka Seltzer, in addition to the usual first aid supplies and shaving equipment.

There was only a bed, a small chest of drawers, and a closet in the guest room, and that was filled with Richard's writing and memorabilia, which Ben sorted through superficially without finding anything that seemed significant. He pulled down the attic stairs and poked around up there, but nothing seemed unusual or out of place.

The dining room was on the other side of the hall from the guest room, and it was full of furniture Richard had inherited (a round, gate-legged table and Queen Anne chairs, and an armoire filled with blue and white china). It looked just like it always had, with a single straw place mat and the family silver, and a book (Boswell's *Life of Johnson*) open on the mahogany stand to the left of Richard's napkin.

Yet the living room was where Richard had really lived, and Ben could almost see him there, sitting in the dentist's chair he'd brought home from England, blowing smoke rings at the ceiling while he talked.

He'd combined the original two front rooms, turning one half into an office that he always kept stripped for work, and the other into a sitting room full of books and records and journals, stacked around two tan chairs and an old leather sofa covered with an African spread.

It didn't take Ben long to inspect the office, to go through the drawers in the worktable, and the picnic basket full of papers, and glance at the books in the bookshelves before turning to the clutter in the sitting room.

The desk Richard used for paying bills was on that side too, and it was another family piece, a tall bureau cabinet with doors at the top and drawers at the bottom and a writing surface in between.

Ben slid his hand across the smooth-polished walnut and smiled to himself as he remembered the wording of the will he'd read that morning. Incorrigible old Richard. He'd left his money to three different charities, but he'd given Ben his Russian icon, his furnishings, his kitchen equipment and all his books, with one stipulation — Ben had to keep his collection of cookbooks intact in perpetuity, or forfeit the rest of the bequest. It was one of Richard's little jokes. He'd been trying to teach Ben to cook since Jessie died, as consciously as Ben had been avoiding it.

Ben sat at the desk and went through Richard's drawers, humming snatches of Mahler's Ninth and something by Bach he couldn't place.

He looked at his watch and put Richard's checkbook in the breast pocket of his trench coat. Then he gathered up five leather books Richard had bound himself, along with the leather-covered loose-leaf notebook he'd found beside Richard's typewriter, and put them in a cardboard box along with one French cookbook and the last two years of Richard West's personal papers.

"Come on, Journey! You know you want to do some work. Hurry up and get over here!"

The chestnut thoroughbred with the four white feet was gazing at Ben across the paddock. If there'd been any grass underfoot he would've made Ben come after him, but as things were, he sauntered toward the gate looking studiously unimpressed.

He walked sedately as Ben led him to the barn, since the wind wasn't blowing particularly hard, and Walter's dogs weren't running around. Journey always tried not to step on people or kick them, even when he was startled by a sudden noise. But he didn't humor them, and he didn't go out of his way to make them feel important.

Sometimes, if no one else was watching, he relaxed his standards. He might let his head rest on Ben's shoulder when his face was being brushed. He occasionally let Ben see that he did like to have his withers scratched; even that rubbing his nose on Ben's chest felt good, when they'd finished their work and he'd had his dinner.

But Ben was different than the ones he'd had before. He couldn't remember exactly what had happened, but he'd learned when he was young that humans take speed and pain and pay you back with neglect. Ben never slapped his flanks with a lead shank when he went into his stall, and he kept clean shavings under his feet, and his meals arrived regularly, which Journey, having nearly starved to death in his youth, knew only too well was the most important thing. There were actually times when he almost liked being around Ben. But that didn't mean that he'd let Ben see it.

"Journey's such a good boy. And you're a very good mover too, aren't you?" Ben leaned over and kissed the soft, delicate muzzle. And then he leaned toward a front hoof, and Journey, having anticipated it, held it up and offered it to Ben so he could pick out the mud on the bottom.

"We have to do the rest of them too, you know. That's right. Now let me brush your snout. There, doesn't that feel good?"

Journey was standing quietly in the cross-ties and Ben was brushing the white patch on his forehead, when Journey lowered his mouth into Ben's upturned hand and closed his eyes and sighed.

The woods were deep with leaves, crackling in the wind and piled against fallen trees. The light was beautiful, dappling the soft ground; pillars of poured light and patches of shade. It reminded Ben of the ruined abbeys of England, the stone cathedrals broken into arches and empty spaces, of light places and dark corners carpeted with moss and soft green grass and grazing cream-colored sheep.

Ben was concentrating on the smells in the woods while Journey twitched underneath him with his head in the air and his ears pointed. He never did relax when they went cross-country. It probably had something to do with being on the track when he was young and having empty space in front of him and being expected to cover it as fast as he could.

A rabbit flew across the path and he bolted, briefly, settling back down to a hot quiver when Ben pulled him up. "It's OK, Journey. Nothing's going to hurt you. Just settle down, and we'll go home in a minute."

Ben's shoulders were tired, and he rolled them backward and forward, while he tried to remember what he'd been thinking about when Journey had lost control.

It came to him eventually and made him

wonder what had happened to his concentration. He'd been trying to place the man Ellen had seen at his desk, the one who'd appeared in the office while Janie was out to lunch, who was good looking and had dark hair and was wearing gloves and had said he was using the phone.

Not quite two hours later, Maggie had seen someone walking around the house, looking in the kitchen windows. His jacket was wrinkled and scruffy looking, which bothered Maggie. And when she'd opened the door to ask what he was doing there, he had beer on his breath in the middle of the afternoon.

Which means what? That the physical description narrows the field. And somebody was looking for something. The only personnel folder in Richard's desk, perhaps?

A lot of people know I'm the executor of Richard's will and have access to his personal effects. Bernard Greene wouldn't have much trouble finding that out, if he wanted to.

But neither would anyone else, and I refuse to jump to conclusions. Who was that criminologist from Mount Holly, New Jersey? He tried more than two hundred murder cases and had a much better conviction record than Scotland Yard or the Sûreté

General of France. Ellis something. Ellis *Parker*. He was the one who used to say, "Facts don't lie. They can only be misinterpreted."

Even though that's not to say that there isn't a place for intuition.

But why did Richard have to be so inscrutable! What did he mean when he said, "You and I are the only people who can incriminate the guilty beast?" And when he quoted Johnson, when I was leaving for England, was that related to any of this?

Not to mention the fact that he could be more circuitous than anyone I've ever met, seeing it as an art form, as he did. If he'd gotten to the point a little sooner, I'd know what I was doing. But . . . life is like that.

"Right, Journey? Come on, let's go home and get your dinner. It's getting dark faster than I thought it would."

CHAPTER FIVE

Wednesday, November 23

"Dr. Ben!"

"Hi, Sarie. How are you?"

"Oh, pretty good."

"May I talk to you for a minute?"

She was standing at the door of a small ranch house, wearing red slacks and a blue fuzzy sweater, with pink foam curlers attached to her scalp like a swarm of slugs. "Of course you can! Now don't look at my hair, I feel so silly! Just let me shut the door to my uncle's room so the television doesn't bother us. It gives him something to do, but he has to keep it awfully loud. 'Course, when I do the dishes, I turn the sound up on my soap operas, so I guess turnabout's fair play, if you know what I mean."

She hurried toward the back of the house and returned a few minutes later, without the curlers, carrying two cups of coffee and a jar of powdered creamer. "I thought you weren't coming back from England till after the first of the year."

"I came back for the funeral. You have heard about Dr. West?" Ben looked at her noncommittally and leaned his head against the high-backed chair.

"Of course." Her lips were working against each other and something closed behind her eyes. "So how can I help you, Dr. Ben? Oh no! Why did I do that?" Sarie had put her wet spoon in the jar of creamer when she'd meant to put it in her coffee, and she was staring at it as though she didn't know what to do.

"I'm the executor of Richard's will so I have access to his papers, and I've been reading Richard's journals and trying to get an idea of what his last weeks were like. Partly because I'm interested, but also because I think something unexpected happened to upset him the night he died. I was wondering if anything he did before you decided to retire struck you as being unusual in any way?"

"I didn't retire, I quit!"

"After how many years? Seventeen? Eighteen?"

"Fifteen in the graduate office and two in the English department working for Dr. West. All I can say is, it happened one too many times and I walked out. How does it go? — 'the straw that breaks the camel's back'?"

She had smooth round cheeks and plump

fingers and soft fuzzy eyes, and with her sensible shoes and her panty girdle making her pooch over the top, she looked like a middle-aged woman waiting for grandchildren to sit on her lap. Except that this time there was hurt and anger and resentment, which Sarie hadn't shown before, tearing at the seams of her face.

"I see. Well no, actually, I don't see. You were very helpful, and very pleasant, and you seemed reasonably content to me, so I was surprised when I heard you'd left."

"I'm not the kind of person who talks about it. I'm the kind who takes it, year after year!"

"I'm sorry, Sarie, but I still don't understand exactly."

"You wouldn't! He was your friend, wasn't he? You agreed with him, didn't you?"

"I'm still not sure what —"

"Do you know what it felt like? My dad organized the plumbers' union in this town. You know what Dr. West used to say about unions!"

"Not all unions, Sarie —"

"My whole life I've looked up to Franklin and Eleanor Roosevelt, more than anyone else I can think of. I hung their pictures above my bed when I was a little girl, and I even stood on street corners passing out pamphlets for Adlai Stevenson until I was so tired I couldn't eat. Well? Do you know what it was like, hearing what Dr. West said about President Roosevelt? That he was 'hoodwinked' by Stalin! That he gave away Eastern Europe! That the Japanese code had been cracked and F.D.R. knew they were about to attack Pearl Harbor, but he let it happen anyway to get us into the war without him having to take the responsibility!"

"Whether that's true, I don't know, but there is a book by the communications officer who —"

"And then he called Adlai Stevenson a fuzzy-thinking liberal! Can you imagine that, an intelligent man like Mr. Stevenson? And all that time, Richard West and Russell Kirk and William F. Buckley were writing back and forth, patting each other on the back! It made me sick!" She was shaking, like someone who's been feeding on hostility and hidden it all her life.

"I'm sorry, Sarie. I had no idea you felt that way. You were always so . . . I don't know how to say it, so —"

"Flustered and nervous? He could shout instructions while he was typing his own lectures and I couldn't even keep up with him in shorthand. Of course he never used a short word when a long one would do, did he? And he'd look at me like I was an idiot and he was being patient!"

"I know he couldn't have been easy to work with, but —"

"I couldn't take it any longer! That last day, he called John F. Kennedy 'the bootleg baby' and I lost my breakfast in the ladies' room!"

"I'm sorry, Sarie."

"I just handed him the note and walked out the door, and for the first time in two years, I slept through the night." She spilled her coffee and wiped it up before either of them said anything else.

"Did you ever tell him how you felt?" Ben spoke quietly, rubbing his hand back and forth on the arm of his chair.

"What good would that have done? He just would've argued with me. It was easier to let him think I agreed with him than spend all day long being hounded."

Her face was twitching and Ben couldn't look at her for a minute. He could see why Richard had made her miserable, and why she'd frustrated him. But he also knew how much Richard had respected her for her kindnesses; for the way she'd made a home for her uncle, and didn't gossip, and managed to get through life without criticizing other people.

"I'm sorry, Dr. Ben, I don't know what came over me. It wasn't your fault, so why should I yell at you?"

"That's all right, I'm glad you explained it. But it's sad too, because I know he liked you, and he respected you for the way you treat people."

"Oh? Do you torment people you like?"

"Yes, unfortunately, sometimes I do. But would you say there was anything worrying him, or preying on his mind? Or did he do anything unexpected?" Ben was leaning forward with his elbows on his knees, watching Sarie pick yarn pellets off the underside of her sleeve.

"No. I quit the week after you left, but I don't remember anything unusual. Keeping in mind that most of what he did seemed peculiar to me."

"Do you know if he was expecting a package? Did he send away for anything?"

"I don't remember anything special. He ordered books all the time. But of course he typed his own personal letters, since I wasn't trustworthy enough to do them properly!"

"Nancy didn't type them either. He thought it was wrong to have a university secretary spend office time doing personal correspondence. So you didn't see him after you quit?"

"Once. I ran into him in the grocery store by the whole-wheat flour." She said it contemptuously.

Ben set his empty cup down on the coffee table and folded his paper napkin. "Anyway, thanks for talking to me, Sarie. I appreciate it."

"Aren't you going to ask me if I have an alibi for Friday night?"

"I didn't —"

"I went to the movies. Alone, as a matter of fact. I saw *Exodus* for the fourth time."

"I'm sorry, Sarie. I'm sorry it was hard for you." Ben was standing beside her, putting on his jacket. "Richard didn't have any idea he was making you miserable."

"He wouldn't, would he? He never gave a thought to anybody but himself."

"It's good to see you, Ben, even though I wish the circumstances were more agreeable. I don't know why, but I still can't believe Richard's gone."

"I know. I can't either." Ben slid his hands in his pants pockets and studied the short, thin, angular man behind the mahogany desk.

"As I mentioned on the phone, Richard's death is what prompted me to get in touch."

"Thanks, Howard. I'm glad you did."

"Please, sit down. Nancy told me you were interested in what his final week was like, and as it turned out, I got what must have been one of the last letters he wrote. It was in my Monday mail, and I thought you might like to have a look."

Ben took the paper Dean Ellis handed him and sat down on the sofa beside the desk. Alderton's dean of men walked to the window and looked across campus with an impassive face that had taken him through years of committee meetings without jeopardizing his advancement in the university, or his place in the academic cliques.

Nov. 18, 1960

Dear Howard,

It is with deep regret that I entrust a matter into your capable hands as dean of men, which fell unbidden into my own.

This evening, at approximately seven forty-five, I was on my way to my office after an excellent dinner (having attempted a French peasant concoction of veal and artichokes I shall share with you at our earliest mutual convenience), when I chanced to pass the Religious Life office.

There I discovered a pair of undergraduates embracing wantonly on the padded bench. Although neither had disrobed, there was a certain degree of sartorial disarray, and their postures left much to be desired — if only in the matter of decorum. In short, you and I would have said they were necking enthusiastically; while they, "the young," if I have the phrase right, would have described it as "making out."

Actually, it was the reek of whiskey which concerned me most. The girl appeared to be too young to partake legally. So I took the names of these hardened reprobates, thinking you might wish a word. Douglas Smith and Susan Putnam live now in a state of unease, which you could do much to encourage.

I presume you may wish to consult the new dean of women, for the female child in particular looked too inebriated for her own good. Perhaps a retributive shock would help protect her from the snares of her own inexperience.

The blessings of an ogre of old.

Yours as usual,
R. F. West

"I assume it wasn't mailed to you?"

"No, he slipped it in my slot. The administration mailboxes are right across the hall from the English department's."

"So he typed it and took it over that same night. Did he often bring disciplinary matters to your attention?"

"Not often, no, but we liked each other's approach. Terrify the barbarians and then offer a reprieve when they least expect it. Assuming they exhibit some sign of remorse."

"Have you talked to either of the students?"

"I've known Doug for some time, but I couldn't find the girl in the student directory, so I suspect she used an alias. Doug wouldn't give me her name either, when I talked to him Monday afternoon."

"Richard probably had her in a state of apoplexy. But I wouldn't mind talking to them myself, if it's all right with you."

"I don't mind. But why do you want to? You're obviously taking more than a casual interest in Richard's death."

"I have to stay here until the will is taken care of and we get his house on the market. And I guess it makes me feel less at a loss to piece together his last days. I don't think anyone has any doubt that he died of angina. The police certainly don't."

"Yet I find myself waiting for you to ask if

he made any enemies while you were gone."

"Do you think of Richard as having enemies?"

"I was being facetious." Dean Ellis had his elbows on the arms of his chair, and he laid the palms of his hands together and then pulled them apart, so only the fingertips touched. "It is true, of course, that he antagonized those of us who are somewhat less concerned with the 'Communist menace' than he was. No, Richard may have been exasperating from time to time, but I wouldn't say he had enemies."

"Was he liked within his department?"

"I'm not sure I can speak with much authority, but aside from the usual academic rivalries, I wasn't aware that there was any particular hostility. Now come on, Ben, I'm not an absolute fool. If there's nothing questionable about how he died, why are you so interested in his activities?"

"You know me. Idle curiosity."

"Or too many years in military intelligence?"

"Maybe. Thanks, Howard. I appreciate it."

Ben was standing in the hall of the S.A.E. fraternity house listening to fifty undergraduates play Ping-Pong and poker and pack their bags with dirty laundry, while threads of music from an extensive collection of radios and record players tangled in the background.

Ben doubted that anyone could study in the midst of it, but then most of them were leaving for Thanksgiving vacation.

They looked so young, these half-naked kids pushing and shoving and screaming obscenities up and down the halls.

"Somebody said you were looking for me."

Ben turned toward the side stairway where a large student in a varsity football jacket was taking the stairs two at a time in disintegrating, sockless loafers. "Doug?"

"Yeah."

"I'm Ben Reese. I was a friend of Richard West's, and I wonder if I could ask you a few questions?"

"Sure. I'm on my way down to campus, so maybe we could stop someplace and let me grab some lunch while we talk?" Doug was tall and blond and had extremely curly hair, and there was something sardonic in the way he met Ben's eyes.

"Fine with me. I've got my car, if you want a ride."

"Great! Have you talked to Dean Ellis?"

"Yeah, he showed me Richard West's letter."

They were halfway down the brick walk when Doug said, "Geeze! Is this yours? What is it, a '48?"

"A '47, actually. My brother restores old cars."

"I've seen it on campus and wondered who it belonged to. He did a great job!"

"*He* says he's a perfectionist, but there are those who think he's obsessed."

"Let me guess, his wife?"

"He also has four daughters."

They sat in one of The Coffee Cup's red plastic booths as Gladys hobbled over with the menu. Doug ordered first (a large chocolate shake, three fries, and two cheeseburgers, loaded), while Gladys, who never wrote anything down, showed Ben a new picture of the nephew she was raising, whose upkeep kept her from retiring.

"How upset was Dr. West when you saw him Friday night?"

"I didn't know him, so I don't have a frame of reference." Doug Smith watched Ben with an expression of unusual intelligence.

And Ben wondered what it was about a face that conveys those things like thought processes. "How would you describe him?"

"Officious. Pompous might be a better

word. Of course, he was definitely outraged."

"Did he have a package with him?"

"I don't think so. I don't remember it if he
did."

"Had he turned red in the face, or was he
having trouble breathing, or did he look like
he was in pain?"

"He was hot under the collar. You know
what I mean, he was obviously incensed. But
for some reason, and I can't tell you why, I
thought he was exaggerating just to intimi-
date us. The girl I was with, she thought he
was so upset he'd try to get us thrown out of
school."

"You didn't, though?"

"No. I've watched what goes on a lot longer. She's a freshman and she's trying to
grow up overnight, but what her parents
think is still a real issue for her. Of course,
now she's afraid we killed Dr. West, and
she's flipping back and forth between feeling
guilt ridden and acting defensive."

"Her name isn't Susan Putnam, is it?"

"No."

"And you aren't prepared to give me her
name."

"That didn't sound like a question. And
you're right, I'm not. If she'd wanted it
known, she would've used it."

141

"True. Although she might remember something you've forgotten."

Doug smiled and said, "Hi, Mr. Campbell."

Ed Campbell was approaching their table on his way to the cashier, carrying a cardboard box full of papers and looking distracted. He said hello to Doug like he was glad to see him, and then smiled self-consciously at Ben as he walked past, as though he wasn't altogether sure who Ben was, but he had reasonably pleasant memories of whatever interaction they'd had.

"Have you heard Campbell lecture, Dr. Reese?"

"No, I haven't."

"I took his Homer course last year and I was impressed."

"Really?"

"Yeah. It's amazing. He's unbelievably shy when you talk to him alone, but when you get him in a classroom, he's a different person. It's like he's been set free from himself. He stops squinting or blinking or whatever it is he does, and I find that incredible."

"That is pretty amazing."

"Yeah. But why are you so interested in Dr. West's last night?"

"He was a good friend and I'm curious. So you aren't going home for Thanksgiving? I thought I'd have trouble catching you."

"No, I've got too much work to do, and it's not that long till Christmas."

"What are you majoring in?"

"I have a double major, history and psychology."

"So what did you think of the election?"

They discussed politics and music and journalism in America while they ate their lunch. Then Ben thanked him for his help and got up to pay the bill.

He glanced back as he opened the door, and he saw the skepticism on Doug's face. The look that seemed to say he didn't believe Ben was only interested in West's last minutes. That it was more than that. And he wouldn't mind knowing what Ben found out.

"Sally Poole?" Ben put the *National Geographic* back on the coffee table and got up from the sofa as a small, thin girl with straight black hair walked out of the elevator in his direction.

"Yes?"

"I'm Ben Reese. I was a friend of Dr. West's."

That took her by surprise, and she sat down in a faded green chair and worked at avoiding his eyes.

"You knew Dr. West?"

"No." She looked at Ben then, at his long legs and his wide shoulders and the obscure expression on his sharp-boned face.

"You met him, though, the night he died."

"Why do you say that?"

"Outside the Religious Life office."

"Did he smoke a pipe?"

"Yes."

"Was he very, very tall, and sort of pear shaped, and was he kind of bald with a ring of red hair around the sides?"

"That is an excellent description."

"I didn't know who he was. Is it true that the last thing he did was write a letter about us to the dean of men?"

"One of the last things."

"Wonderful! I mean, do you think we killed him? Was he so upset he had a heart attack because of us?"

"I don't think so, no. He was upset. He called me in England before he died, but I don't think it had anything to do with you." Ben leaned against the back of the sofa and laced his fingers together behind his head. Then he smiled at her, because she looked serious and worried and tired of her own deception. "So why have you decided to tell the truth all of a sudden?"

"I hate lying, and I feel ridiculous. I've

known Doug for years, and that Friday was my birthday. He isn't my boyfriend or anything, but he took me out to dinner and I got a little drunk. I normally don't even drink much beer, but they didn't ask for an I.D., so I had two whiskey sours. And then when Dr. West found us on the bench, I panicked. My father's on the board of trustees here, and I guess I just chickened out. It's different now. I mean, your friend died that same night, and I'd feel horrible if we had something to do with that." She'd dropped her lighter and Ben picked it up, sliding the ashtray toward her across the table.

"I don't think you had anything to do with it. But I wonder if you could describe him for me. Was he red in the face, or sweating? Was he carrying anything? A package maybe?"

"No." Sally blew a stream of smoke toward Ben and stared at the ceiling as though she were trying to see Richard's face. "When he was yelling at us, he turned kind of red, but it didn't last long. I don't know what else I can tell you. He had his pipe out. And I think he was carrying a briefcase tucked under his arm, but I don't remember a package. I was feeling pretty fuzzy myself, so I don't know if I would've noticed."

"Women in any condition usually notice

more than most men. At least in this kind of circumstance. Anyway, I appreciate your help. But try to behave yourself, OK? So you don't have these embarrassing memories to live with." Ben laughed and laid his right ankle across his other thigh.

"I'm glad you can laugh, because I can't! How'd you find me, anyway? Doug didn't tell you, did he?"

"It seemed to me that a person who was making up an assumed name might have a tendency to use one that began with the same letters as their own. I also had the impression that Doug had met your parents, so I checked to see where he was from. You were the only freshman woman whose last name began with *P* and whose first name began with *S*, who also came from Arcanum." Ben smiled and stood up and said, "Thanks again, Sally. Take care of yourself, OK?"

Sally Poole watched Ben run across the lawn in his desert boots, and his cords, and his old English jacket, with the wind tearing at his hair. It was the kind of brown that turns blond in the summer, and it was fine and straight and shiny. She liked his mouth and his Adam's apple and the way his eyes crinkled when he smiled. She liked the boniness of his face and the way he'd looked at her, as if he understood what she liked about Doug. That was very strange. It was almost as though he'd known her a long time. And then she thought, "But do I get professors like that? No. I get lunatics like Grace Giardi!"

Ben drove his car into the small barn he used as a garage, then slid the doors shut behind him and looked at the woodpile on the back porch. It was enough to get him through two or three days, if a snowstorm took out the electricity the way it had in '55. That's what had made him think about putting a Franklin stove in the house when he'd moved to town. You could cook on it and melt snow to drink if you had to.

He'd already cut and split two and a half cords out at Walter's, and he ought to get the last one into town. But he wanted to restack the pile behind the garage and add the seasoned wood to the back porch first. And he ought to cultivate Maggie's vegetable garden too, before the ground froze solid. Maybe he'd do that after dinner.

"Dr. Ben?"

"Hi, Maggie. What's up?"

"I'm on my way to my daughter's." She was wearing a heavy black coat and high-laced shoes, and her maroon 1940 felt hat with the feather on one side (and when she took it off, her hair would stay plastered against her scalp like she had a stocking stuck on her head).

"How's your car?"

"It's starting OK. It must've just been the battery. But before I forget, President Cook called. He wants to know if you'll have Thanksgiving dinner with him tomorrow in some restaurant. I told him I'd have you call him when you got back. 'Course if you want to have him here, I've got plenty in the house. I'll be eating at my daughter's, but I thought I'd fix you a turkey breast. Tonight I'm just baby-sitting. I ought to be back before ten."

"It'd be nice to eat at home. You sure, though? It's not too much trouble?"

"Of course not! I planned your dinner before I went to the store. If I left it to you, there wouldn't be bread in the house!"

"Now that's something of an exaggeration."

"Sure it is. Anything you say."

"That's why you never get chosen for jury duty."

"I beg your pardon?"

"Your biases are too conspicuous."

"No, you're just trying to change the subject! Don't you remember me telling you that I wish you'd entertain more?"

"Vaguely."

"Do you remember what I did before I retired?"

"Well . . ."

"Just as I thought! I managed the Columbus Women's Club, and I oversaw all the catering. I'd like to have a chance to show off once in a while. Even if it is President Cook."

"Now, Maggie, that wasn't nice."

"He's such a phony!"

"Not really. He's just trying to make up for having —"

"Never mind. I'm sorry I said anything."

She wasn't, though. Ben looked at the expression on her face and laughed.

"OK, so would you rather have the cream of cauliflower or the curried consommé?" Her pocketbook was over her arm and she was pulling on her gloves, but Maggie was watching Ben's face like a lawyer with a hostile witness.

"Now wait a minute, *you* have to do the menu. You know much more about these things than I do."

"You want him for dinner or a late lunch?"

"I don't care. Whatever's easier for you."

"An early dinner? Five or five-thirty? I can get it ready, and then go to my daughter's in time to help her."

"Fine with me. Thanks, Maggie. What would I do without you?"

"You'd eat peanut butter sandwiches in peace and quiet and you wouldn't mind at all. Oh, I almost forgot! David somebody called. I didn't write his name down, 'cause I was mopping the floor at the time. But he asked me where you keep your horse. I told him about Walter, and he wanted his address and phone number, so I gave it to him. I hope that was all right. He said he'd call back later."

"That's fine. Thanks, Maggie. Say 'hi' to Missy and Tom."

Ben was lying in bed with Richard's last journal propped on his chest. He'd finished both volumes from 1959, and he'd also looked through the notes for the novel. It was interesting, seeing Richard's interior life. Although the journals weren't diaries in the usual sense. They were stream of consciousness explorations of whatever he was thinking when he picked up his pen.

But Ben felt like he was prying, and he never would've done it, except for the circumstances of Richard's death.

6-20-60 — It would have been

Mother's birthday today, and it's pitiful, how little I remember her, although what can't be changed shouldn't be brooded over. Still, since I wasn't quite seven when she died, I suppose I can't help but wish that there had been more of her influence in my life.

Odd, the habits one develops. Last night, as I was trying to get back to sleep, I began thinking about that trip to Greece and wondering where I should go this year (in view of my reduced circumstances), when I suddenly noticed that I was typing the word "vacation." My big banana fingers, in perfect touch-typing position, were gently tapping it out on the mattress on either side of my large, reclining carcass. It occurred to me then that I've been doing that, fingering the odd word unconsciously, for almost as long as I can remember, when I suddenly realized how idiosyncratic that probably is.

Then I began wondering what sorts of similar activities other people might do without intent. Do jockeys, watching the sunset on their day off, find themselves holding nonexistent reins in their hot little hands? Do burlesque queens manipulate imaginary feather-fans in empty elevators? The possibilities are endless and really quite intriguing! And may well be worth considering as I work on my novel.

I remember Bill used to tie knots in midair. And Jim twists a lock of hair around an index finger in public. But what does he do in private?! What would Sarie do, I wonder? Or Dr. French? Naturally, Bernard deserves an unleashed imagination, but I shall refrain from further contemplation. I refuse to even venture an uncharitable guess, after the first eight chapters of Corinthians . . ."

Ben put the book down on the wooden trunk and turned off the light. It was late. And he was tired.

What was it Richard had said in his next-to-the-last volume? "Logic is the fruit of reason; meaning is the child of imagination."

Ben had never felt a conflict between the two and he doubted that Richard had either. Any more than either one of them had seen a conflict between reason and revelation.

But there had been one moment as he read the journal, when he'd imagined Richard turning to gaze at him over his shoulder while he lit his pipe. It was nothing alarming.

Just some form of déjà vu.

And although he couldn't have explained it, Ben had the feeling, reading those entries, that if he'd been able to ask Richard, while he was writing those journals, who would have murdered him (if such a thing should ever happen), Richard could have told him. Not because of circumstance. No. Because of character.

CHAPTER SIX

Thanksgiving, November 24
"Delicious, Ben, simply delicious! Your Mrs.
Parsons is a woman of taste. You know,
sometimes I actually envy you."

Jim Cook was leaning back in Ben's
wicker chair, pulling his suede sleeve down
over a monogrammed cuff.

"Really?" Ben was wiping cranberry and
orange sauce off the front of his fisherman's
sweater, wondering how much longer it
would take him to finish Richard's journals.

"I love Mary Ann and the children very
much, and I miss them every day they're
gone, that goes without saying. But once in a
while, it is nice to live your sort of life. You
do what *you* want to do, without anyone
complaining or interfering or telling you
what you should be doing, in their unbiased
opinion! . . . Oh, Ben, I'm sorry. I forgot. I
never met your wife, so I —"

"I know what you mean. And you're right,
on that level. So what can I do for you, Jim?
Something's on your mind and you're being
subtle."

"Well. Now that you mention it. You

know how much we need new lab space, a place to undertake serious scientific research, physics and chemistry and —"

"Do we? Dr. Jarvis isn't complaining, is he? I know Harry Welsh was telling me that he's ordered quite a bit of new equipment, and I thought he was satisfied with that."

"But the old chemistry lab! It really won't do, Ben. It does not give the impression of fiscal well-being, and attracting good faculty, as well as alumni support, depends on making a good impression. You have to admit that Warren Hall is inexpressibly ugly, and it —"

"But it does what it was designed for and it's in good condition. The enrollment's steady. There aren't any new demands there. We've got a great faculty-student ratio. And I think our money should be going into faculty and equipment."

"Then how can we compete with the state schools?"

"We can't in size and construction projects, but we can provide things that they can't. At least *we* still have academic standards. And there's real interest and rapport here between the faculty and students, and that's much more important than more buildings. At least to me. We just built the astronomy and geology building, and I don't think the alumni are in any mood to be milked."

"*That's* why I wanted to talk to you! I was glancing at some of the cataloguing you've done. You know, the artifact lists you've compiled over the years with the estimated values for insurance purposes. And it looks to me like we're sitting on a gold mine."

"I beg your pardon?"

"Think, Ben! Just the coin collection old Peabody Edwards donated in the twenties — I mean, how much is that worth?"

"You mean to tell me you'd sell the antiquities! The rare books and the paintings? The coin collections, and the pioneer diaries, and the maps and land grants that were given to us?"

"Of course not! Not all of them. Just isolated items from time to time."

"Then that won't bring in enough to build buildings. Jim, the men and women who held on to those bits of history wanted students here to be able to appreciate them. I thought you were once a historian!"

"I still am. But we can't keep living in the past; we have to think of the future."

"I am thinking of the future. I'd like to have tools with which to work. Something to pass on. Something that's worth preserving."

"Well. I can certainly see why you'd feel that way. And it's nothing that has to be decided now. I just thought I'd bring it up."

"Did you discuss this with Richard?"

"No. He was an English professor. It wasn't his province."

"But you did see a copy of his report on Bernard Greene?"

"Yes, it was on my desk Friday morning."

"And you supported Richard's decision to dismiss him?"

"Let's say I didn't interfere. I might not have handled it the same way, but he acted within the bounds of his own authority."

"I see. How would you have handled it?"

"Ben, I hate to eat and run, but I have to get to work on an alumni speech. I'm trying to gather support for another small modernization, although far be it from me to expect encouragement from my friends! Only the students are unhampered by 'what has been before.'"

"What modernization is that? And by the way, I'm thirty-eight years old and you're making me sound like a dinosaur."

"Sometimes you act like one! Living like a recluse can do that." Jim laughed as he said it, while he felt his pockets for his car keys. "I was referring to our Methodist affiliation. I think we should distance ourselves a bit. Of course you wouldn't agree I'm sure, as their state historian."

"They give us a small amount of financial support, and provide a counseling office and a part-time minister. I don't think they make undue demands. I oversee historical research for them, yes, but I'm not a Methodist. I'm deliberately nondenominational, and no one's ever mentioned it."

"Why do you use the drafting table?" Jim had stopped just inside Ben's library door and was peering at the table as though he were evaluating its aesthetic qualities.

"I pace when I write. I work in pen and ink once in a while too, and when I'm trying to decipher an illegible document, being able to get it up on an angle is easier on my eyes."

Jim had picked up a book from the center of the sloping surface and was sliding his fingers along the edges as though the feel of it was somehow comforting. "This is beautiful leather."

"Richard bound books. That's one of his journals. He was writing a novel too. Did he mention that to you?"

"No. Who would have thought?"

"It takes place in a graduate school, and it examines the ways in which different people react to the pressures of academia. He hadn't started the actual writing, but he must have been close."

"Richard, the Renaissance Man." The notebook slipped off the drafting table as Jim laid the journal down, and he bent to pick it up with the unhurried economy of a cat. "Well, Benjamin. Thanks again for dinner. I'll have to swim three miles tonight instead of two!"

"Any time. Goodnight, Jim." Ben closed the door and turned his back to it, gazing absently up the stairs.

So what do I do to keep Alderton from selling the collections? Repossess the archive lists first, probably. And then insert subject notes in the card catalogue that say information on university collections can be obtained from the department of archives. That should give me time to think about what to do next.

Ben wiped off the table and took the dessert dishes into the kitchen, then he scraped the plates into the garbage while he ran hot water in the sink.

Grace Giardi slid hangers from side to side looking for her rose wool suit. The peony print blouse was there, but where was the suit? "*Mon Dieu,* but it has fallen on the floor!" It was lying tangled among her oldest shoes back in the corner in the dust. She

159

shook it out, brushing it off with a plump white hand, and began picking at specks of lint while she talked.

She'd been talking out loud for years when she was home. But there had been two or three times recently when she began to think people on the street were looking at her oddly, and she'd been terribly afraid they could hear her thoughts.

And that was before Richard had passed away. It had gotten worse since then. She had more trouble remembering where she was. The conversations she carried on with him made things confusing. Teaching was all right. She knew where she was when she was teaching. Reading the great writers: Rousseau. De Maupassant. Balzac. Mauriac. Zola. Who was it that wrote *Madame Bovary*? "How is it possible that I should forget! I, who understand it so physically and so completely! No. It is indeed my memory, as I have feared." And why do I prefer French writers to the Italian, to my own native tongue, to my own papa's compatriots? Except of course the opera! Now there the Italians reign supreme. Those Germans, I can only laugh. "Only laughter would be polite!"

Yet perhaps it is a literary prejudice, brought on by my own misfortune. Perhaps having been abandoned, I condemn

Alberto's comrades unfairly? A topic I must consider seriously at a later date. "But now, I must enter the world once more! I must not let myself grieve unduly. I must be strong! I must seize life in my own two hands!"

She slipped her blouse over her head and struggled with the buttons behind her back. "Oh, *Mon Dieu,* that it should be so snug is not possible!" Didn't I wear it to the symphony with Richard? Yes, and it was not what you would call loose then. But that was sometime in the summer. It was hot then, the wool suit. But I was glad of it in the air conditioning. I remember remarking of it to Richard at the time.

"Well. So? If all the buttons cannot be buttoned, it's not a matter of such great importance." The jacket will cover it, after all. Ah, but what of the skirt? The zipper, it half-way closes, almost. But there is little hope of the waistband meeting. Such is the way of the world! "Yet . . . the jacket is long, and it will suffice. If one's standards are not unduly high, *n'est pas?*"

She had reached an agreement with her mirror some years earlier. When she spread on the heavy cream or the tan liquid that filled her pores and smoothed away the wrinkles, she would gaze at the glass without her glasses to gauge the effect. Also with the rouge, and the eye shadow, and the eyebrow pencil, and the mascara. But once the thick round tortoise-shell glasses were in place, she never faced the mirror again. The peony lipstick went on by feel, seeping away from her lips in the fine cracks around her mouth without her ever knowing. And her own naked body she hadn't seen in its entirety since 1953.

"But where shall I dine? Elegance is a pre-requisite, of course, and yet in such a town! Hahh!" In such a town it is preposterous! If Mama could see what I have come to, she would weep. Mama with her porcelain skin and her tiny feet. Such a time she had! Such a longing for those days with Papa! So? Per-haps the Imperial House? "Yes. They at-tempt the *coc-au-vin*. And the bartender, *he* is a man of feeling!"

Ben had washed the dishes and lifted weights in the basement while listening to Miles Davis, but his mind kept coming back to Richard's journals. Even more than the notes for the novel, it was there that Ben saw him and heard him. He took a cup of sassa-fras tea into his study and lay down on the sheepskin rug, leafing through forests of strong black script, looking for the place he'd stopped.

11-1-60 — Bill has been on mind many times this past week. I'm plotting the novel, and my graduate school experience is therefore uppermost in my thoughts. He had such innocence, William Taylor, and he took such enormous interest in his work.

Of course, Bill's forte was never human nature. Unlike David Krause, who was able to criticize everyone around him with a painfully insightful eye. Bill saw what was best in all of us, and there was something humbling in that for a person of my sort — a man who recognizes vice and selfishness, having lived with them intimately all my life.

I, of course, would be hard pressed to re-live a single moment of our walking expeditions through the Indiana hills in my present state of corpulence. I can see it in Ben's eyes: his memory of what I was, in comparison to what I've become. Not that Ben would ever refer to my adiposity! Oh no. He's far too discreet. And he reveres the right of every American to make a fool of himself in his own way (as long as he doesn't impinge upon anyone else's right to do the same).

The gratifications of food are so immediate; that's the crux of the problem. Slimness, on the other hand, has to be planned for and worked at like an army maneuver. Perhaps the time has come to outflank myself (puns ever were my weakness). And perhaps I'll think about it tomorrow — like Scarlet O'Hara.

I wonder if Bill's parents are still alive. I haven't talked to them in years. I do wish he had had the opportunity to publish his dissertation. Having uncovered that excerpt of Timothy Flint's diary, he was able to shed considerable light on the battle of Trenton, while contributing to our understanding of both General Putnam and General Washington. Yet Bill died before he could share his perspectives with the scholarly world, and all of us have been lessened by that.

What does indeed weigh heavily, is that I talked Bill Taylor into enlisting. By my very temperament, I simply cannot resist trying to influence other people's opinions. I have no doubt that he would have enlisted sometime; but if it had been later, if it had been another branch of the service, if he had been sent anywhere else — he wouldn't have been on his way back to England after escort duty on a B-24 bombing run, not on March 7, 1944, and his P-51 wouldn't have been shot down by a Focke-Wulf east of Bordeaux. (And why is it that writing those statistical particulars makes his death seem more concrete, and, therefore, easier to accept?)

I realize that my feelings of guilt are pointless as well as wrong. The God of falling sparrows was watching over William, and the fall of that plane was acceptable to Him.

It's *my* involvement in it I wish I could change.

Then too, I suspect Sarie's note has taken its toll. How could I have been so oblivious? There was such animosity, such venom, such vindictiveness on her face! Yet I have no doubt that I was to blame — at least in part. Sins of omission, as well as commission.

For I have certainly been insensitive to other people's convictions in the past, and yet I haven't learned from it! I misinterpret a lack of rebuttal for agreement, apparently. I would never hear an opposing viewpoint expressed without presenting my own, and I assume no one else would either. Perhaps she's intimidated by verbal confrontation? Perhaps she thought her job would be in jeopardy if she stated her opinions? That never would have been the case, and yet how was she to know? The intricacies of a retiring nature have always been (and I fear, shall remain) a deep and abiding mystery.

Ironically, and probably pathetically, I thought Sarie liked me. I wanted her to. I liked her. I have a great need to be found acceptable to women. And yet I fear it too. Perhaps it has to do with my mother's death. And Glenna certainly. Always Glenna.

It's astounding what a spectacle I make of myself without even trying. Think what I could do if I applied myself!

11-3-60 — Grace Giardi is a very persistent woman. I have no intention of establishing any sort of intimate relationship with her, and yet I feel sorry for her. I hope I will be able to continue to escort her here and there at carefully spaced intervals, for her own sake, without her reaching inaccurate conclusions as to my intentions and state of mind. She has fine sensitivities, and kind feelings in many ways, but she is indeed unstable and unbelievably myopic (in every sense of the word). The poor woman has made her bed in never-never land. And all I can hope to do is diminish her loneliness, at distanced moments, without having to avoid her altogether.

Tricky, Richard old boy. Very tricky.

Of course Jim is another interesting case. A man of clear-cut goals at the very least. It's interesting how knowing a person a long time both complicates and clarifies one's feelings about them. If I didn't remember how self-conscious and shy he was in college, how frightened he was of seeming gauche or inexperienced, of using the wrong fork, or pronouncing a word incorrectly — I would be sorely tempted to be brisker with him today, in all his newfound splendor. I can still see him, much incapacitated by gin at age twenty-two, telling William that in junior high he'd been ridiculed for smelling of cow dung after morning milking, and how he had subsequently developed an elaborate ritual-ablution to keep it from recurring. His temperament has somehow fed upon those early experiences, so that it is very difficult for him to do anything without worrying about how other people will react to him as a result.

Still, before the war, there was a sort of well-meaning obliviousness in Jim, and a certain openness to the metaphysical, but . . .

"Hello-o? May I come in? Dr. Reese? Are you at home?"

"Yes. Just a minute. Miss Giardi! Please, come in."

She had already opened his front door and was wavering on the threshold. Ben had a very accurate nose for alcohol, and she smelled of scotch. It seemed to him that her whole body had taken on its distinctive odor.

Her face was white with powder, her lipstick was leaking around her lips, and she'd drawn black Egyptian eyes around her own, which were so magnified by her lenses, it looked as though two brown egg yolks were floating in a pool of oil. Her auburn hair was disturbing too, very thin and too often dyed and curled, and she plucked at it with long, varnished red claws, the same way she worked at the collar of her blouse and her string of yellow pearls.

"I so hope I do not intrude, but you see I knocked, my friend, and no one answered. And yet I could see the lights in your front windows, and hear the music as well."

"No, I'm glad you came. It happens all the time. I lose myself and I don't hear a thing. May I offer you a cup of coffee, or tea?"

"I wouldn't dream of imposing! You see, I've sought you out because I understand you're investigating Richard's death." She said it in a hushed, throaty voice as though she were touching on a matter of great secrecy.

"I'm not sure I'd use the word *investigating.*"

"Then you should! It is my considered opinion that he was murdered, Dr. Reese. Yes, that is indeed the word, *murdered!*"

"Why, Miss Giardi?"

"No, no, no! You must call me Grace. Miss Giardi makes me sound such an old woman. You see, I spoke to him that last night, just before he died. Ah, my friend, I hate to bother. But would it be possible that you should have a drop of brandy? I begin to feel quite fluttery inside my chest." And she did light her strong European cigarette, a Gitaine probably (she took it from a gold case and he couldn't be certain), with a slightly unsteady hand.

He'd forgotten she had an Italian accent. What was it Richard had told him? Her father was an impoverished Italian nobleman, and her mother had been an English governess? Something ludicrously romantic like that. Maybe her mother was American. "I don't think I have any brandy, but let me make you some coffee or tea."

"Thank you, my friend. You are too kind, but I fear it would keep me awake. What was I saying?"

"You talked to Richard the night he died."

"Yes. Yes. And I have a strong, strong conviction that his death was not natural. That somehow he was brought to it with cunning. You would say that this is an instinctual reaction, because I have no proof that it is so. But I feel it in my heart, and the heart has its knowledge too!"

"When did you speak to him?"

"I rang him while he was cooking. We chatted for a while about the symphony and the performance of *The Messiah*, which the Choral Society is preparing for Christmas . . . No. Such an act is too ignoble. Please forgive me. For what I have said is not true. I did not wish to appear too forward. The truth is, I dropped by his house, as I have yours. Dinner was always the best time to run him to ground, as it were, while he was cooking and planning his evening. And that night we agreed to see a film the following afternoon. I'd thought perhaps we could do so later that same night, but he was anxious to visit his office."

"Did he say why?"

"No, he did not. Of course he often went back at night. But he did make a remark which I did not understand, and which seemed particularly significant to him. That although he had spent his life studying human nature, even he was surprised by the self-interest exhibited in a matter he had lately uncovered. 'A significant contribution' he called it, 'in the annals of human ambition.' "

"Did he explain what he was referring to?"

"No, he did not. But he added something about having been placed in a position to correct an injustice. If his suspicions proved to be true. But you see, when I asked Richard what he meant by that, he laughed and changed the subject. Did you not find that he did so effortlessly? One never was able to persuade Richard West to say more about himself than he wished to reveal."

"Did he give the impression that there was a specific reason for going back to the office that night? Was he planning to meet someone?"

"I don't know. I do not know. I have lived a life of abandonment, Dr. Reese. I will say no more. I would not wish to embarrass you with my little troubles. But the future, Dr. Reese, without our dear, dear friend, looks very bleak indeed. You see, we had come to an understanding in recent weeks. And my loss is greater than it was before. I can say no more." She looked tragically at the rug.

And Ben wasn't sure how to react. "I'm sorry. I miss him too. I knew him a long time."

"I must go. Be diligent and do not forget his unyielding loyalty to those who won his love, as you did!"

"I'll try. By the way, did Richard leave anything with you? Any papers or photographs?"

"No. No. Good night. Oh! There is one thing. You know of course that Dr. French hated him, and was jealous of his great connections in the literary world, as well as his successes here? Oh yes! You see, Dr. French was passed over for the chairmanship which Richard was awarded, and he never forgave. No. He never forgave! Good night."

"Do you have a car?"

"No. I walk."

"I'd be happy to drive you home."

"No, my friend. The cold is a great comfort."

She disappeared down the street, her small, overburdened heels irregularly pecking at the pavement. Her green coat burst into view under a street light, only to be swallowed by the darkness between them, until the brow of Worcester Street hill covered her, finally, like the night.

Ben stood outside Patsy's Bar and Grill and looked at his watch. It was a few minutes after ten and the interior was filled with noise and smoke and hot bodies crushed against each other, leaning over the long, dirty bar or packed into cramped booths. Ben opened the door, and the heat and the smell rolled over him like a wave of foul water, as he worked his way toward the bartender underneath a large neon Stroh's sign. "Excuse me. Is Bernard Greene here?"

"He was. Give me a second." The large bald head swiveled from side to side as the hands poured drinks and wiped the counter and stuck swizzle sticks in glasses without pause. "Like I say, he ain't in here right now, but he lives upstairs. You go up there by the outside door. Front apartment. You can't miss it."

"Thanks a lot."

"Sure. Happy Thanksgiving."

Ben looked to see if that meant anything and couldn't decide. He walked out onto the sidewalk, turned, opened the peeling wooden door, and started up the dark stairs.

There was a bare bulb hanging from the ceiling at the top, but he didn't see any name or number on the two doors. He knocked on the one closest to the front and waited, but nothing happened. It was standing slightly ajar, and he stuck his head inside and called; and then he finally pushed against it and walked into an unfurnished room.

"Bernard? Is anyone here?" There was no answer, but there was music coming from the back, and Ben threaded his way through abandoned bags of fast food and dirty ashtrays, until he was standing in a small, squalid bedroom.

It was dark. Chuck Berry was playing on an old hi-fi. A girl was lying face down on a mattress on the floor, her arms around a wadded sheet. "Hi. Who're you?"

"Ben Reese. Is Bernard here?"

"He was. He'll be back in a minute. I'm Rena."

"Hi, Rena. You OK?"

She sat up and leaned against the wall, and it looked as though she was holding herself up with one hand, while the other one fumbled with a pack of cigarettes.

"Here. Let me do that." Ben pulled out her last Winston and lit it before handing it back.

She let the hand that held the cigarette fall across her knee, and then she propped her head against the wall to hold it still. "You ever drunk boilermakers with peppermint schnapps?"

"No."

"Don't."

Ben heard someone moving in the living room, and he turned toward the hall.

A man ran into the bedroom, rushed past

Ben without looking at him, and dove head first through the open window in the back wall.

Ben started after him, as Rena laughed, and then the man's head reappeared in the opening. The face was laughing uncontrollably with its chin lying on the window sill. "Man, you shoulda seen your face! Hey, Rena, what'd ya think? Very cool, right?"

"Bernie threw a mattress out on the roof, 'cause a friend of his was gonna stop by, and Bernie thought —"

"Knock it off, Rena, he'll figure it out! . . . Geeze! I can't get up! Can you dig it, I can't climb up! Give me a hand, will ya?"

Ben stuck both hands through the window and pulled the dead weight of a drunken body off the high, flat roof.

Bernard slid down the wall until he was sitting on the floor, tapping a Lucky Strike on his thumbnail and trying to focus on Ben's face. "So do I know you? Wait! You're from Ohio State, right? No, don't tell me, let me guess . . . I know I've seen you around . . . somewhere . . ."

"I'm Ben Reese."

"No kidding!" He took a drag on his cigarette and started giggling, snorting the smoke out his nose in little bursts. His face was slack and unfocused, but then it changed — the dark eyes and the good bones and the well-made mouth — into something more cunning and suspicious.

"I think it's time Rena went back to the dorm, don't you? Then you and I can have a quiet talk."

"Oh yeah? Who do you think you are! Get outta the way, Renie, I'm gonna teach this creep a lesson!"

Bernard was standing, weaving on his feet, staring at Ben in the semidarkness with his fists hanging limply at his side.

"Don't, Bernard. You're too drunk. Just sit down and take it easy."

Bernard lunged toward Ben, but Ben closed his esophagus with his good hand, while turning Bernard around and twisting his left arm behind his back.

"If I were you, Rena, I'd get back to the dorm. Go on. Right now. You have an illegal I.D., and you could be expelled for what Dr. West saw. Listen to me! OK? Right now!"

She got up on her hands and knees and rested. Then she stood up and stayed there, swaying, looking at Ben as though she wanted to say something.

"I'm trying to help, believe it or not. You have to go, Rena . . . Wait, you dropped your purse. Careful on the stairs. OK?"

Bernard's back was still toward Ben, his

arm twisted behind him, his body pushed against the wall, his head turned to the left. He tried to kick Ben in the crotch while Ben was watching Rena, but Ben tightened his grip and shoved Green's head against the wall again, hard, staring down into his one visible eye as though he were examining an infected rat. "You're going to stand here, perfectly still. Aren't you, Bernie?"

"Let go of me! OK! OK! That's enough! I forgot, alright?"

"You wanted to look for something in Richard's office, didn't you? And when you couldn't get in, and you found out that I had his papers, you began to think maybe it was in my office. You were interrupted there, so then you tried my house. Only to be lectured on the evils of drink by a woman who could've been your grandmother. Poor Bernard! You were hoping he hadn't had time to do anything. He saw you Thursday, and he died Friday, so you thought maybe you'd been lucky. It's too late, though, Bernie. Dr. West's copy of the report was in your file in his desk. President Cook got his Friday morning. And you should have the paperwork in the next day or two."

"He came in here and found us in bed. I mean, he just walked right in without knocking!"

"He knocked. The door was open like it

was tonight and you just didn't answer."

"I'll tell ya one thing, if I'm in his novel, you can bet your rear end I'm gonna sue, you hear me! Who's his publisher?"

"How'd you hear about the novel?"

"He was a stuffed shirt! I mean really, man, he was so square it made me want to puke! What business is it of his what I do in my spare time? Huh? Tell me that! What business is it of a bunch of prehistoric jerks who I sleep with!"

"If the girl is a student and underage, I'd say it was a matter the university has a right to consider. I wouldn't be surprised if the police might be interested too."

"Wouldn't you! And who do you think you are?" Bernie started to struggle.

And Ben shoved his head against the wall again and tried not to let himself enjoy it.

"OK, just be careful, all right?" Bernard's chin had started to tremble, and his shoulders began to shake.

Ben loosened his grip without letting him go.

"I can't lose this job! I've got debts from school and I've gotta have the money."

"There are other jobs besides teaching."

"All I want to do is be a professor! You can dig that, can't you?"

"Yeah, but professors have to control their behavior."

"I got nowhere to go! I just gotta have this job, man. You gotta understand that!"

"Maybe you should've thought of that earlier. You can't seduce college girls and be allowed to get away with it."

"You and Richard West! You got all the answers, don't ya?"

"No. Where were you Friday night?"

"Columbus. I was in Columbus."

"Alone?"

"No! I spent the night with my girlfriend. I got there about seven and we went out to eat and I spent the night."

"What's her name?"

"Pat Strachan. High Street and Edgerton. South side. Top floor on the left."

"What's Rena to you then, if Pat's your girlfriend?"

"Nothin'. Somebody I shack up with once in a while. I told her. She understands. She has a good time."

Ben let him go, and Bernard slumped against the wall with his mouth hanging open and his eyes blurred and bloodshot.

"Well. At least Rena's luck's about to change."

"Oh yeah?"

"Yeah. You'll be out of here in less than two weeks."

CHAPTER SEVEN

Friday, November 25

The house sat on the side street like a body cast that's been cut off or an empty egg case washed up on a beach. And yet it made Ben think, as he stood looking at it in the dawn light, that once, when it was young, it was clean and cared for and filled with the enthusiasms of little kids.

Now the siding was stained and the curtains were hanging dejectedly, and Tom Price was standing in uniform on the porch, and it looked like any other public scene of despair.

The neighbors were clutching their coats over their bathrobes on the walk, or peering out their windows with cups of coffee in their hands, out of human curiosity and human detachment, and the relief of watching it happen to someone else.

Ben didn't look at them any more than he had to, while he snaked his way through toward the porch.

It was almost disconcerting how much the inside of that house looked the way he would've expected, with its small wallpapered

180

rooms filled with flower patterns and faded drawings and undistinguished prints of Europe. The tables were cluttered with mementos: framed photographs of family and friends, small pieces of statuary, inlaid Italian boxes, porcelain eggs and engraved letter openers lying idle, as well as European fashion magazines and literary journals.

The overstuffed pieces were mostly sagging and floral. The lamps were old-fashioned and formal with tasseled and tucked silk shades. The wooden furniture was Italian, some of it Renaissance, heavy and dark and elaborately carved.

Yet it was the sense of order overlaid on dust and dirt and staleness that struck Ben — the lapsed cleanliness in the face of filth, straightened on the surface to cover a core of decay.

"Morning, Ben. Sure didn't take you long."

"I'm glad you called me, Chester."

"Yeah, I figured maybe you would be."

"How'd she die?"

"Asphyxiation, most likely. Choked on her own vomit. Caused by alcohol and sleeping pills, from the looks of it." Chester was standing with his hands on his hips and a toothpick between his teeth, gazing at his men across the room.

There were two of them in their shirt-sleeves sprinkling white powder on dark surfaces and dark powder on light and then photographing the results, with their cameras set on pocket-sized stands. Next they'd lay Scotch tape down so the print could be lifted off the surface and stuck on a labeled card, before they set a small magnifying glass above another, in order to compare and evaluate it.

"Has the coroner been here?"

"Just left. Have to wait till the autopsy to find out if the barbiturate-alcohol levels would've been lethal. Looks self-inflicted, but whether it was suicide or accident, we don't know. No note, anyway."

Grace Giardi had died on her own sofa, surrounded by rose-covered cushions edged with lace. An ashtray had overturned on the floor beside her, spilling crimson-smeared cigarette butts across the rug. Her hand hung above the mess, above the overturned glass with the lipstick stains and the spilled scotch. And a half-bottle of prescription sleeping pills stood on the end table beside a third of a fifth of Johnny Walker Red. The front of Grace's housecoat was splattered with vomit. Her short swollen legs were twisted underneath her, and one small foot stuck awkwardly out in front, as though she were a rag doll who'd been tossed across the room.

"Any sign of a visitor?"

"Nope. Not so far. Why?"

"She came to see me last night. I guess it must've been between eight-thirty and nine. She'd probably had two or three drinks, but she seemed reasonably under control. Anyway, she came to tell me she thought Richard had been murdered."

"Oh yeah? She say who?"

"No. Unfortunately. But she talked to Richard the night he died, and he'd said something about having been 'put in a position to correct an injustice,' if his suspicions proved to be true. Of course she had no idea what he meant by that. But she was convinced he was murdered because of it."

"That's pretty much what Richard said to you. He didn't explain it any better than that though?"

"No. Except that he said he was 'surprised by the degree of self-interest,' in whatever it was he'd uncovered. Although she did mention, in passing, that Dr. French was jealous of Richard. But only in general terms. He was the only person she could think of."

"She looked real unstable at the funeral. Remember?"

"I think she was unstable. She was certainly emotional last night. It was almost like she saw herself as a great romantic heroine who's been ill-treated by the fates. And of course, she could have been suicidal. Richard's death was a real blow. But as you said before, people O.D. and asphyxiate themselves accidentally." Ben locked his fingers together on the top of his head and stood staring at the window behind the sofa. Then he cocked his head sideways, and looked contemplatively at Chester. "Don't you think she would've taken more sleeping pills if it had been deliberate? She left half a bottle."

"Could be. We'll have a better idea after the autopsy, how much she took. Have to see when she renewed the prescription too. The label's stained where the date is."

"I know instinct is dangerous, and I have no idea how to explain it, Chester. But it seemed to me that she enjoyed the melodrama too much to end it. But what do I know about her? I only talked to her four or five times. Although Richard told me about her, in general terms."

"He never mentioned her to me. 'Course he didn't talk about his personal life hardly at all."

"I think she got on his nerves. And yet he felt sorry for her. He was trying to avoid telling her she was beating a dead horse, without encouraging her by not saying it." Ben was quiet for a minute, standing with his arms crossed and his eyes on the bookcase across the room. "Would you mind if I looked around? I won't be offended if you'd rather I didn't."

"No, go ahead. I gotta get back to my notes anyway." Chester introduced the lab people, then walked into the hall and sat down on the chair beside the telephone table, before picking his clipboard up off the floor.

Ben slid the leather cover off his magnifying glass and examined the body in great detail. He read the prescription label, the "Nembutal 100 milligram," on the bottle of yellow capsules. He lay down on the floor so he could study the area rug, and the ashtray, and the mess around it, before the police had a chance to vacuum. He spent a long time on the overturned glass. And he inspected the furniture, and the walls and woodwork, before he looked at every painting and print and photograph.

He stayed out of the technicians' way as much as he could. He worked quickly and he apologized and walked around them. But when he stopped in the doorway and stood there with his eyes half-closed and his jaw off to one side, both of them were watching as though they didn't want to distract him, any more than they wanted to look too interested.

Or so it seemed to Ben, when he felt them staring at him and turned and caught their eyes.

He finished the molding around the archway that led into the hall, and scanned the floor to the front door. He examined the handle, then opened it with a handkerchief and studied the lock and the sill, before pacing back and forth across the covered porch with his eyes on the painted floor. He contemplated the positions of the neighboring houses while Tom made conversation, and then he stepped inside and walked past Chester, straight toward the back of the house.

The kitchen was small and neat, but it was cluttered with odd pieces of memorabilia: a Cinzano ashtray, a tiny white china urn with pastel flowers, a donkey with panniers that might have come from France, and a collection of empty Chianti bottles, most of them wound with raffia. There were dishes stacked in the sink, waiting to be washed, but methodically organized according to size. There was a large water glass, two dirty juice glasses, and a stack of three small plates

— the bottom one covered with toast crumbs, the middle with a small patch of egg and coagulated grease, and the top with what appeared to be salad dressing and tomato seeds. Corresponding pieces of silverware lay on the right beside a worn omelette pan and two cocktail glasses — one containing diluted milk, the other empty, except for a fraction of an inch of water. Ben ignored the large water glass and the juice glasses, and examined the other two.

"Chester?"

"Yep?"

"Can you come here a minute?"

"Sure." He was making sucking noises between two teeth and fishing a toothpick out of his shirt pocket as he came through the door. "What's up?"

"Look at this."

"Yeah? So? It's an empty highball glass."

"It looks clean."

"Yeah."

"Isn't that inconsistent? Look at everything else. Organized neatly and rinsed superficially, but still dirty. It looks to me like this one's been washed with detergent."

"Could be." Chester took his glasses off and rubbed the place where they sat on the bridge of his nose as though it hurt, then he pulled a handkerchief out of his pants pocket and rubbed his lenses before he leaned over and looked again.

"It wouldn't be as significant if the water weren't so hard. See how it streaks and accumulates in large drops on the juice glasses, and that tall one over there? Even the plates. Look how irregular the dispersal pattern is. There's a very high level of mineral salts in our city water, and it averages forty-grain hardness. Most of the wells are even worse."

"Yeah, I have to bring in bottled water."

"I had to too, on Poe Road. But this glass is covered by an even sheet of water, with hardly any streaking, or drop formations."

"OK. I can see that. So where does that take us? You think somebody was here, drinking with her? And washed the glass to get rid of his fingerprints?"

"It's worth considering. The front door-knob wasn't wiped, but it's cold enough now to wear gloves without attracting attention. You could sit in an upholstered chair without leaving a trace. And you can also set a glass down without putting prints on the table. Of course, the vacuum may turn up hair or fibers or something more. But with a glass . . ."

"I'll get 'em to fingerprint the kitchen. Course on a wet glass it'll be easier to find traces of detergent."

"I thought the one in the living room looked too clean too. There aren't enough prints, and the ones that are there are too perfect. It's almost like there isn't enough smearing and overlapping. That make any sense to you?"

"Yeah. It looked like it to me too."

"I know what I meant to ask you. Who discovered the body?"

"Paperboy. Got here about five forty-five and saw the door was open. Not much, six inches maybe. So he went up to close it, but then he stuck his head in and called Miss Giardi in case she'd left it open on purpose. He saw her on the sofa, through the archway there on the right."

"Poor kid! How old is he?"

"Eleven. Name's Jimmy Miller."

"Would you mind if I read his statement?"

"Fine with me. Remind me before you go. I sent him home right after I called you. Smart boy, though. He walked over to that telephone table and told the operator to get the police."

"Is he OK?"

"I expect he will be. Anyway, I must've called you about fifteen minutes after I got here."

"Why did you? Nobody else would have." Ben's hands were on his hips and he was fac-

189

ing the back window, but then he turned and looked at Chester.

"I tell ya, Ben, I just kept seeing the expression on her face, when she was standing at Richard's grave. Don't get me wrong, I'm not convinced the deaths are connected. But I figured you might want to know, and maybe you could help, being acquainted with both of them. I mean, two professors in one week? People who know each other?"

"Exactly. What's the coroner say about the time of death? Rigor hasn't set in yet."

"Not before midnight. Probably not before two. Rectal temperature, taking into account the temperature of the room and the amount of clothing she was wearing, makes him think it was right around 2:00 A.M." Chester had slid his hands inside his trousers on either side of his belt buckle, so that his thumbs hung over the edge of the wide, heavy belt, and he was staring at the clock above the kitchen stove. "Funny thing, after all this time. Bothers me more when it's a woman. Can't explain it. Don't make much sense."

"I know. And I don't understand it either. You see any reason to think there's anything missing?"

"Not that we've noticed. Course that's hard to say. 'Specially in a case like this."

"You want to run through the rest of the rooms while we talk?"

"Yeah. Sure. You go first, the hall's kinda narrow. Talk louder when you aren't lookin' right at me."

Chester watched Ben study the door to Grace's bedroom, thinking he looked different than normal. He'd never known Ben too well, of course. Just casually. Just well enough to shoot the breeze once in a while. Knew more about him from Richard, really, than firsthand. He appeared to be real easy-going and unhurried, usually. Like he did things in the right order, without letting himself get rushed but without being too picky either. He wasn't prissy or phony or strung too tight, like some of the university people. And he never gave you that smug look a lot of Alderton folks used when they talked to "townees." No, if somebody had asked him, Chester would've said Ben was an outdoorsman of some kind. You could picture him with a fishing pole or a pitchfork or washing his clothes in a river.

But now he was moving fast. Real directed and efficient and cold. His eyebrows were pulled down tight, but his eyes were covering ground, and he made you believe he wasn't missing much. Maybe it came from the war, but he looked like a hunting animal. Like a big cat or a blue tick hound or something. Even the bones in his face looked pointier than usual.

"I don't see anything in the bedroom, or the bathroom, or the guest room. Unless you noticed something?" Ben paused and looked at Chester as though he wanted to fulfill every possible obligation.

Chester hadn't met too many police chiefs who would've allowed Ben to be there. And quite a few might have resented the way he went along on his own like he did. But Chester had a soft spot for the truth, a real serious respect that had come to him as a boy. Even then he couldn't stand by and watch anybody be lied to or teased with an untruth. Of course he'd never been ambitious to speak of, either, not for himself. His father never had liked that about him much. Not that it mattered to Chester. He admired facts. Impersonal facts. Even if the cleanness and the hardness and the edge of them hurt, and made his job as hard as any. There was nothing relative about the truth in his line of work. It pleased him and contented him, like few things did. Except maybe tracking deer in the hills in the early morning. Not to shoot, unless they were starving. Just to track. That was some sort of truth to him too.

So whether it was him or Ben who got to the bottom of these two deaths didn't matter to Chester Hansen.

At least not much.

"I don't understand it, Chester."

"What?"

"I don't see anything to indicate it wasn't suicide, or accidental death. Nothing but the glasses even raises the question. But I'd bet my Napoleon plates she wasn't alone when she died, any more than Richard was. No, I think there's a brain at work here, Chester. A very careful, self-protective, long-range planner. Sitting patiently. Watching two human beings die painfully before his eyes. Or hers. It could be a woman, absolutely."

Chester reached in his pocket and adjusted his hearing aids, while he asked Ben what it was he'd said about Napoleon.

"What?" Ben looked at Chester as though he'd never seen him before, but then recovered himself and apologized as he examined the inside of the linen closet. "After Napoleon declared himself emperor, he made his twelve field marshals dukes and commissioned a set of plates to be designed with a different ducal insignia on each one. He had three complete sets of twelve handmade by the firm of Capo de Monte. And today, there's one set, in excellent condition, in the Louvre, and another, that's badly damaged, in the British Museum. I bought the third four years ago in a junk barn in South Carolina, complete and in perfect condition, for thirty-six dollars. Don't you think it might be interesting to know if the neighbors saw anybody coming or going last night?"

"I sent Roberts out half an hour ago to begin the preliminary questioning." Chester was smiling by the door when Ben looked over at him, as he dropped the guest room bedspread and got up off his hands and knees.

Ben Reese knew Craig French; at least he'd met him several times. The most memorable occasion having been when Ben overheard him in a record store, telling one of his poetry students that he'd heard C. S. Lewis speak on medieval poetry when he'd come from England on a lecture tour. Ben knew for a fact that Lewis had so far never set foot on American soil, and his estimation of Dr. French had plummeted as a result.

"Is he in, Nancy?"

"Dr. Reese! I didn't hear you come in." She clutched her heart first, then pulled off the earphones to her Dictaphone machine, while nodding in the direction of Dr.

French's door. "He got here about fifteen minutes ago, and I called your home but no one answered. I've got Dr. Richard's mail ready for you to sort through too."

"Thanks, Nancy. Is it alright if I take it with me?"

"Just bring back anything that has to do with the department."

"Would it be OK for me to see the last two phone bills?"

"Fine with me. Dr. West always went through them too, so he could pay for his personal calls." Nancy lowered her voice and raised her eyebrows in the direction of the closed door across the hall. "If there're any objections, I can truthfully say that the chief of police asked me to cooperate with you, the way I would with him."

"I appreciate it. And while I'm thinking about it, what's the name of the janitor?"

"Albert Weber. His 'offices' are in the basement."

"Thanks, Nancy."

Ben knocked on the heavy wooden door and waited. A thin, peevish voice said "What?" as though matters of urgency were being thwarted.

But Ben opened the door and walked in.

"Oh. Dr. Reese. Come in. May I offer you a cup of coffee?"

"I'd appreciate it, if it's not too much trouble. I've been walking all over town, and it's getting cold."

"Nancy? . . . Ah, there you are. Would you bring Dr. Reese a cup of coffee please?" He kept his eyes on the door, until she'd walked in again and performed her function, and then he said, "Thank you. Too kind. Where were we?"

He was sitting in front of a metal stand full of shriveled violets and dry-looking ferns. And he reminded Ben of a cockatoo, picking at his papers with his sinewy hands, jerking his bony, sparsely covered white-haired head from side to side as he talked and watched Ben with undisguised irritation, while his eyes strayed occasionally to the open book in front of him. "To what do I owe the honor, Dr. Reese? I somehow doubt that this is a social call from one gifted scholar to another. For it goes without saying, that I have heard something of your activities, and if this concerns the death of my departed associate, I fear there's nothing I can say of any interest."

"I did wonder if you might have been working late yourself the night he died. If you'd heard anything, or seen anyone going in or out of his office?"

"No. No, I was attending our latest theatrical effort, and reviewing it for the university's . . . how shall I put it? The university's 'attempt at journalism.' I entitled it 'Our Town: Revisited One Too Many Times.' Perhaps you read it?"

"No, I was in England, and only got back Sunday for the funeral."

"Too bad. It was rather well received, I thought."

"Do you remember if you collected your mail last Friday?"

"Yes. Sometime during the afternoon. Certainly before my four o'clock class."

"I don't suppose you happened to notice whether or not Richard had a package in his mailbox?"

"Hmmm. Yes, now that you mention it, I did. His slot is directly above mine and I had difficulty working a journal past the obstruction."

"Did you notice what it looked like, or where it came from?"

"I am not in the habit of examining other people's mail, Dr. Reese. All I can recall is that it was an ordinary brown-paper parcel. Perhaps two or three inches thick, and long enough to stick past the end of the pigeon-hole."

"I take it you weren't very fond of Richard?"

"He was an ambitious, hypocritical prig. He was intolerant and simplistic and a great bore. He insisted upon viewing the world as a combat zone, if you will, in which the forces of clearly delineated righteousness and evil contend with one another in some perpetual cosmic conflict. Righteousness and evil writ large in letters of stone, no doubt. He perceived every decision he and this department made as skirmishes in the 'greater battle,' and he viewed all political activity in a similar light. Picturing himself, of course, as a champion of right, and goodness, and of God and his brightest angels.

"I, on the other hand, perceive existence as something quite different. A matter of chance and absurdity. Perhaps even a study in futility. So that questions of intent and purpose appear ludicrous to me. And his obsessive punctiliousness was frankly nauseating." Dr. French turned a letter opener over in his hands as he talked.

And when he met Ben Reese's eyes, the coldness made Ben wonder if his life hadn't already become a misery to him.

"Of course, as you must have learned from more than one willing source, he was awarded the chairmanship of this department when I had served it longer, and some have even said, more ably. And my personal indignation consequently knew no bounds. I speak frankly, because I see no reason whatever to posture. I'm far too old for such obscurantism, even if I had the patience. And I'm too close to retirement to be given another chance at the position.

"But was I involved in the circumstances that led to his death? No. He killed himself with his own silver-pronged fork. And a more fittingly ironic end I couldn't have planned myself."

Ben wasn't sure whether his own pity or disgust had the upper hand, but Craig French's face made him want to leave him there alone in his tufted Edwardian chair. "Well, thank you, Dr. French. I'm sorry to have bothered you. Oh, one other thing I meant to ask. Did Richard tell you he was writing a novel about a university?"

"Was he? I was hardly a confidant. But if so, I have to assume it was satire. He would never have been capable of creating rounded, realistic characters. No, Richard West would glorify people like himself, and caricature those with whom he disagreed. It's a dangerous game, wouldn't you say? One which frequently ends with a libel action in a court of law."

Ben was standing by the door watching Craig French with his hands in the pockets of his corduroy pants. "I was surprised to find that Bernard Greene knew Richard was writing a novel."

"Did he? That's intriguing."

"I thought so. And I asked myself why Richard would have told Bernard, when they seemed to have a generally hostile relationship. Especially since Richard had told me he wasn't going to mention it to anyone."

"And am I to know what answer you came to? Assuming that you came to any."

"That he didn't."

"I see! So how did Bernard uncover the information? Telepathy perhaps, or interrogation under torture?"

"Curiosity, probably, to begin with."

"If you do actually wish to communicate, Dr. Reese, perhaps you could make an effort to be a bit less obscure."

"The day I left for England, Thursday, October 27th to be precise, you had breakfast with Richard at his home, and I think you looked through the notebook for the novel that he kept on his worktable in the living room. Maybe he was getting breakfast ready, or cleaning up afterward, but he'd left you alone. And once you realized what you had in your hands, you didn't like the idea of Richard writing about academia. I think you were afraid you'd see yourself from his perspective, and so would everyone else. And then when you told Bernard Greene, he didn't like the idea any better than you did."

"I've listened to quite enough of your unsubstantiated accusations for one day, Dr. Reese, and I'd appreciate it if you'd do me the courtesy of allowing me to get back to work."

"Of course. Good-bye, Dr. French. Thank you for the coffee."

Ben took the three flights of stairs to the basement fast, wondering whether there'd been more fear or hatred in Craig French's eyes when he'd pushed him about Richard's novel. He also asked himself whether either reaction actually meant much. There was no hard evidence, obviously. And there wasn't much of a motive that could tie French to Richard's death. Aside from a general dislike and a not very unusual outbreak of professional jealousy. Plus an ill-defined fear of being caricatured in Richard's novel.

Unless, of course, Richard knew something really damaging about French that French would kill to keep quiet.

Richard wouldn't do that — reveal something publicly that would injure someone. Not unless it was an ethical issue. Like a "travesty that deserved retribution."

But of course, Craig French wouldn't know that. Not with his view of Richard's character.

And either way, French wasn't a simple person. He was quite accomplished at presenting a constructed image of himself when he chose, and he'd know how to cover his tracks.

Ben worked his way through a warren of storage areas and heating ducts and plumbing pipes, until he found a door to a small room standing open next to the main boiler. It was very hot, and there were rumblings and hissings and a rhythmic mechanical rattle where a gray metal desk sat surrounded by mops and buckets and commercial brooms.

A small, very thin man, with wispy hair and glasses and a tiny mustache, was leaning against the desk, lighting a cigarette and looking out the door at Ben.

"Mr. Weber?"

"Yeah?" He was staring at the center of Ben's chest and he seemed to have trouble deciding where to put his hands.

"I'm Ben Reese. I was a friend of Richard West's."

"Yeah?"

"It sure is warm in here."

Mr. Weber didn't say anything. He flicked

the ash off his cigarette and stuffed his hands in the pockets of his khaki pants.

"They say we're supposed to get hit by a big storm this weekend, and it's already snowing. But you don't have to worry about feeling the cold in here."

"Yeah, well, the wife told me not to come in. You knew I just got over pneumonia? Yeah, three weeks in the hospital flat on my back. Better than the blood clot last year. 'Cept they wouldn't let me smoke." He started coughing and it sounded like a lung was on its way up. But when he finally caught his breath, he took a deep drag on his Pall Mall. And then when he exhaled, nothing much came out; just a trickle of smoke from one side of his nose.

"Actually, I was wondering, Mr. Weber, if you were here last Friday night? The night Dr. West died."

"Yeah. Yeah, I was. First week back on the job. I was coughin' up lots of phlegm, but I figured, what the heck? As long as I took it easy, it'd get me out of the house, right?" He looked at Ben knowingly and rocked back and forth on the balls of his feet.

"You didn't happen to see anybody in the building, did you? Anybody at all? Anytime in the evening?"

"Maybe. What if I did?"

"Who, Mr. Weber?"

"I already talked to the police."

"Chief Hansen told me you hadn't seen anyone. But you know how it is, we all forget all kinds of things, little details that slip our minds. I thought maybe you might have remembered something since. Just hearing somebody on the stairs even."

"I can't say what time."

"That's all right."

Albert Weber didn't say anything more for a minute. He stared nervously at the door and smoked his cigarette.

"Please, Mr. Weber."

"Why do you want to know?"

"I think Dr. West had a visitor shortly before he died and I'd like to know who it was."

"Guess maybe whoever it was ain't talking? Am I right?"

"Yes."

"I don't want any trouble. It's hard enough around here, what with nobody appreciating how much you gotta do. Never satisfied, some people. Dr. West, he wasn't satisfied easy either. Course he could laugh. He was friendly, when he wasn't real busy."

"Please, Mr. Weber."

"I guess maybe I seen a couple people that night."

"Who?"

"Dr. West. Seen him on the stairs. Sarie dropped by too. Seen her sitting at her old desk in the outside office there, when I was dry-mopping the hall."

"Was that before or after you saw Dr. West?"

"I don't know. I wasn't paying attention. She wasn't the only one, neither. The grouch was here too. You know who I mean. French. Set his wastepaper basket out in the hall when my back was turned, like I don't get to it fast enough to suit him. I wasn't about to neither, not till Saturday in the A.M.! Tuesday, Thursday, and Saturday, and I ain't gonna change to coddle him!"

"Did you see him face to face?"

"He had his door closed, but I heard him on the phone. I got real good ears."

"No idea what time, though?"

"Don't wear a watch. Cuts off your circulation. Course I got home at nine forty-five, so it was before that. I watch wrestling at ten." He had another coughing fit and Ben looked away out of delicacy. (Although it also occurred to him that maybe it was time to throw away his Camels, even if he did smoke only one or two a month.)

"Did you hear any raised voices or any disturbance?"

"Soon as I finished mopping the floors, I went down in the basement to clean up my supplies. You know, check the boilers and get ready for the big clean on Saturday. So I didn't hear nothing. Nothing but what I told ya already."

Ben had made himself a cup of coffee and taken it into the study, and he was looking out the window across the fields to the far woods, contemplating the works of men.

"The rattle of the world," as Aleksei Tolstoy called it. But then, he was a poet. And at least as obsessed as his cousin Leo.

It was the squalor of Grace's death, and his own distaste at the waste of a human life — that was part of it.

But it was more than that too. There was a hot, frustrated irritation that came from something he couldn't place.

His library was a kind of sanctuary, ordinarily, which was why he'd gone in there. It fit him like an old flannel shirt or the right-size mug. There was satisfaction in the white shutters and the window seat, with a fire in the fireplace and a comfortable chair, and the records and books that took him off into places of the intellect — into other times and other countries and other people's minds.

But that night, it was making him uneasy. It was almost as though he'd forgotten something important he should've done. And he shivered in front of the glass, seeing his reflection on a night world of dark blue snow, like his own uselessness in the face of death.

Maybe I haven't seen something I should have that would've kept Grace alive. Or maybe it's exactly the way it looks, and there's almost nothing to go on.

He glanced at his watch and wondered why it felt later than six-thirty. Not having eaten anything today except an apple is probably part of it. I ought to make a sandwich and reread the last section of Richard's journal. Chester should be done with the shift change by then, and I'll call him at home and tell him what Weber said about Sarie and Dr. French.

And that French lied too. That was interesting.

But Richard's journal wasn't on Ben's drafting table, and it wasn't next to his chair. Ben felt sure he'd left it in the study somewhere. Although he could've taken it up to the bedroom and forgotten about it.

But it wasn't beside his bed, or on Jessie's

desk, or on the floor by the rocking chair.

And it wasn't in the living room, or the kitchen.

Which didn't make any sense. He'd read it in the library after he'd gotten back from Grace's. He'd put on Beethoven's Fifth, and sat down to read the last three entries. He'd had the novel notebook too. He'd laid it on the floor next to the lamp.

Ben stood in the doorway and looked at his library. And then he saw that the shelves had been rearranged.

All his leather-bound books were gone: Shakespeare, Johnson, Donne, Milton, Trollope, Tolstoy, Austen, Pascal, Dostoyevsky, and Chaucer.

And so was Richard's last journal and the notebook for his novel.

Blast.

Ben ran upstairs again to see if Richard's other journals were still in his walk-in closet, in the box behind his shoes, with Richard's bills and checkbooks and personal papers.

They were still there where he'd left them, apparently undisturbed.

"Is a tuna fish sandwich and tomato soup OK?"

"Sure. I called the wife on the way over. She's real easygoing. Except on our anniversary. Says it's like being married to the only doctor in town." Chester took one last look at the library, as his lab people started on the shelves, then he followed Ben into the big brick kitchen and nodded toward the Franklin stove. "Lucky you got that thing. It's supposed to get bad. Four inches on the ground already and it's coming down faster all the time."

"It's too soon, Chester. I'm not ready for winter."

"Let's just hope it's not like that blizzard in '55! 'Member that? Buncha old folks froze to death."

"Didn't a truck driver die too?"

"Snowplow driver. Broke down and then lost his way trying to find a house. Where you keep your spoons?"

"Top drawer on the left side of the refrigerator."

"So the guy at the newspaper says French turned his review in after the Thursday night dress rehearsal instead of Friday night, like he said. Yeah, I'd say that's pretty interesting!"

"But not conclusive."

"Right. Course Weber heard him too. So whatta ya think? Someone after Richard's diary? Or somebody stealing rare books?"

"If they were after books, they don't know

much. I didn't have anything that was really valuable, just secondhand editions picked up at random." Ben stirred the soup on the stove and then put bread in the toaster.

"Careful, the way he rearranged your books."

"Yeah, if he hadn't, I would've noticed what was missing a lot sooner. And it was definitely premeditated. Maggie got a call from the principal of her granddaughter's school, saying she was sick and they couldn't reach her parents. But when she got there a little after one, no one in the principal's office or the infirmary knew anything about it."

"Ralph Benton's the principal over there, so it must've been a man who called. Right?"

"That's another thing. The secretary or the nurse would've phoned, not the principal. But that didn't occur to Maggie at the time, she was worried about her granddaughter. And she was only gone forty or fifty minutes, so we've got the time down."

"She upstairs?"

"No, she's baby-sitting in Columbus this weekend for her son and daughter-in-law. I told her to go ahead, that you'd talk to her later. I hope that was OK?"

"Just give me her phone number before I go. Kinda odd isn't it, that they'd have school the day after Thanksgiving?"

"I think it's just the nursery, or the nursery school, or whatever they call it. If I remember right."

"So it was set up by somebody who knows your situation here pretty good. Your comings-and-goings, and Maggie's family, and all and everything. Who knew about Richard's journals?"

"Ah, the very question I've been asking myself. I mentioned them to Sarie. And I discussed the novel with Craig French this morning, although *I* think he already knew about it. He would've had to get on to it awfully fast, though, because I didn't leave his office until after eleven-thirty. I have no reason to believe he knew about the journal, but anyone could have found it once they got here and started looking. As of last night, Jim Cook knew about the journals and the notebook for the novel. But Richard could have mentioned them to anybody, theoretically. He could've changed his mind after I went to England and told all kinds of people about the novel." Ben had been staring at the inside of his refrigerator while he talked.

"Yeah, except he told you he wasn't going to, and he made you promise not to either. Were you looking for the mayonnaise? Or the celery maybe?"

"Both. Thanks, Chester."

"So who else knew about them for sure?"

"Bernard Greene. He mentioned the novel. He thought Richard had already written it. You see, French could easily have seen the notebook for the novel at Richard's house when he had breakfast there in October, and I think it's very likely that he's the one who told Greene. That's only supposition, though. There's no evidence whatsoever."

"We got to get to it sometime here, Ben. I mean, what have we got in the way of motive? Or method even, for that matter. One death by angina, one death by asphyxiation induced by alcohol and barbiturates. Both those are natural causes, up to a point. If you figure Richard and Grace were helped on their way, we gotta get to the why and the how of it sometime. And what's any of it got to do with this burglary? If it does. Yeah, and how'd the guy get in?"

"I leave the kitchen door unlocked except when I go to bed. I know! You don't have to say it."

"You gotta be kidding me!"

"It's a small country town, Chester. Most people leave their doors unlocked, just like when I was a kid. Don't you think?"

"Well, I wish they wouldn't! It's getting so

you can't anymore, and it makes my job a whole lot harder, I can tell ya."

"So anyway. Several people could've been afraid that Richard had made derogatory remarks about them in the notebook for the novel, or even in the journal. It wouldn't have been difficult to deduce that I was the person who had them, either. Sarie and Jim knew I did. And all three of them, French included, might have wanted to destroy them, if only for personal reasons. Bernard Greene too."

"So you're saying somebody might have wanted the journals out of circulation, or the notebook for the novel, who had nothing to do with the deaths?"

"It's possible. But of course, the murderer might've thought he had a lot more to fear than embarrassment." Ben pushed his chair back from the kitchen table and propped it against the wall, rubbing the scar across his left palm absently with his other thumb. "I think Richard discovered something extremely incriminating about someone here, and whoever it was confronted him and then let him die. Maybe he even goaded Richard into an attack and then kept his pills away from him, I don't know.

"But if that's true, then perhaps whoever it is thought Richard had told Grace about it too. When she came here last night, she said she and Richard had 'come to an understanding.' And yet I know that wasn't true. I read his journal right up till the day he died and he talked about how he felt. He was trying to be nice to her and keep her at arm's length.

"But if she got carried away and told the murderer, not having any idea who he or she was, that she knew what Richard was doing, and how he was going to set right an old wrong — which is pretty much what she said to me — the murderer, with the booze and the sleeping pills right there, might have thought it was worth a try. He could even have known she was here and have been afraid she'd told me everything she knew too. Or would sometime, even without realizing what she was doing."

"Course we couldn't find any trace of her sleeping pills in her drink. But there was somebody with her, Ben. At least part of the night. I meant to tell ya earlier. Mind if I get me some more soup?"

"Of course not. Here, let me have your bowl."

"Edgar McClosky, next door on the east side? He was up taking a Gelusil for his dyspepsia about eleven. Saw a man walk up to Grace's door. Couldn't see his face. He wasn't real tall and he wasn't real short, and McClosky'd never be able to identify him. But he saw him alright. First real substantiation we've had. Also, unless his girlfriend in Columbus is lying, Bernard's alibi checks out for when Richard died. She looked pretty unshakable to me too. But what I wanted to ask you was, did the journal or the notebook say anything incriminating about anybody?"

"Not that I saw. He talked about how he felt about certain people. How he evaluated their characters. But there's nothing concrete that implicates anybody directly. Unless I missed something. A code maybe. Richard worked in decoding. I don't know. Whoever it is probably didn't know what was in them before he took them. Presumably. And I don't expect fingerprints in the library either."

"Nope. This guy wears gloves."

"He couldn't wear them when he was drinking with Grace. But I bet he washed his glass after she was dead."

"Right. We heard back from the lab, like I said. No fingerprints, but the cocktail glass in the kitchen was washed with a lotta detergent. There was even more on the one in the living room, like whoever washed it was in a hurry. It was too neat too, like you said, with the prints being so clear. Not enough of 'em either, if she'd been drinking all night."

"Then I'd say whoever was here was after the journal and the notes for the novel, wouldn't you?"

"Yeah. And the rest of the books were a blind. But why was Grace's door left open?"

"Could've been unintentional, of course. But if it hadn't been open, her body probably wouldn't have been discovered until Monday, until she failed to show up for class. Maybe he had a reason for wanting it to be found sooner?"

"He won't hold onto the books. He'll have to dump 'em or burn 'em maybe. But I know one thing, Ben. This guy's getting nervous, and you must make him pretty uncomfortable. Know what I mean? Richard called you in England. You've read the journals. You're asking questions. And Grace Giardi came to see you the night she died."

"I know."

"I'd like to leave Tom Wilson here tonight, after we finish."

"Thanks, Chester, but I don't think you need to. I ought to be able to take care of myself."

"Yeah, well, you can't stay awake forever."

"I'm the kind of person who wakes up

when the neighbors whisper, unfortunately. I've also got a .45 upstairs, and I know how to use my hands. They can be deadly too, as I'm sure you know. The manipulation of certain pressure points. The right blow to the throat or the base of the skull."

Chester thought Ben's tone of voice was kind of peculiar.

But then Ben laughed.

And Chester let it go. He just told Ben to keep his doors locked for once, while he toyed with the idea of leaving somebody to watch the house without saying anything about it.

Of course, Ben would notice if he did. And Chester couldn't bring himself to go behind his back.

CHAPTER EIGHT

Saturday, November 26

The wind was shaking the house and rattling the windows, and the snow was peppering the glass like buckshot. Ben could even hear it in the basement, where he was restoring a painting he'd picked up that fall — a primitive frontier portrait of a man in a frock coat that was worth about a dollar ninety-eight.

Yet there was something appealing in the serious eyes and the quiet mouth. He rubbed day-old bread across a small square in the upper right corner (and then watched it crumble and carry off years of dirt) and thought how even that light a cleaning is still a subjective process. The same way that deciding what to retouch, and what sort of pigments to use, are all equally important and equally a matter of personal taste.

He was half-listening to the FM station when they announced it was four degrees above zero and there was a foot and a half of snow on the ground. The wind was already forty miles an hour and increasing steadily, and the snow was drifting dangerously. The state highway patrol was requesting that all but emergency vehicles stay off the road.

Ben could feel the house holding on against it. When he got upstairs and looked out the windows, snow was blowing horizontally and coming down so hard he couldn't see anything else. He brought another load of wood in from the back porch, and then he filled the buckets and the sinks and the upstairs tub in case the electricity went out and he couldn't pump more water. He hunted around for flashlights and candles and put them on the counter, and then he settled down at the kitchen table near the wood-burning stove.

Ben liked being snowbound, as long as he had food and water and could stay warm. He loved watching a fire, and being able to paint or putter around, or just sit and think and read books because he felt like it.

But that afternoon he sat in his director's chair, with his thumb on one side of his jaw and his fingers sliding along the other, thinking about ambition and pride and how they make people defensive. How you can end up wanting to avoid reality in favor of pretense, and appearance, and self-protection.

He'd been thinking about what Richard had said when he talked to him in England, about there being "an unseemly degree of ambition in this particular quarter."

Quarter meaning "culprit." Or so he assumed.

And that led Ben to think about concrete instances of ambitious behavior, while he dug his wallet out of the back pocket of his Levi's and laid it on the table. He sat still and stared at it, then picked it up and passed it from one hand to the other, as though the leather felt good and he was thinking about something else.

Then he opened it and pulled a piece of plain brown wrapping paper out of an inside pocket, a small, jagged scrap perhaps two and a half inches by three. The one he'd found in Richard's office behind an empty wastepaper basket that Albert Weber hadn't touched.

Ben studied it as though he wished it could speak and laid it on the table. He stretched his arms over his head and laced his fingers together behind his neck, and then gazed at the ceiling with half-closed eyes.

Richard had opened a package sometime after eight o'clock, and called Ben in England at nine. That was something of an assumption. But some sign from the outside world had arrived between the time he'd seen Grace and the time he'd called Ben, which had convinced Richard that whatever he'd suspected was true. He wasn't carrying a package when Campbell and the others saw him at eight. And with the scrap of wrapping paper, and the brown-paper parcel French saw in his mail slot, it was a reasonably logical conclusion.

So if that were true, then the person who was with Richard when he died had taken the rest of the wrapping paper as well as the contents of the package.

Not necessarily, though. The door was unlocked Saturday morning, so someone else could've come in and taken it. Although there was no reason to believe that's the way it had happened. Because it wasn't a random relationship, Richard's death and the package's disappearance. No, there was cause and effect involved.

And when Ben found out what was in that package, he'd know why someone had wanted Richard dead. And when he knew why, he'd know who.

Sarie had been there. After having lied to Ben, she'd told Chester she'd gone back to her old office the night Richard died to look for a fountain pen her father had given her on her twenty-first birthday. She admitted she had a duplicate key to the department office she'd "forgotten to give back." And she said she hadn't told the truth to begin with because she didn't think she'd be believed.

And that could be all there was to it.

But she'd also been hugging hate inside herself for a long time. And that eats away at spirit and usually leads to some kind of death — physical or spiritual or both.

Craig French hadn't told the truth either. He'd been in his office Friday night. And none of them had a substantiated alibi for the time of Grace's death — not French or Sarie or Bernard Green. They were all home in bed, alone.

And they may well have been. Both murders could have been committed by someone I haven't considered, much to my own disgust.

Assuming they can technically be called murders. We can't prove that Richard's medication was kept from him, or that Grace's pills were dissolved in her Scotch. So we've got to come up with something concrete or we won't even get it into court.

And of course, with plea bargaining the way it is, it could end up as voluntary manslaughter anyway. And then what? Even if whoever it is is charged and convicted of first degree murder, convicted murderers are paroled every day. Especially now that the death penalty's become suspect.

Ben wiped the lunch crumbs off the table and threw the dishcloth into the sink more heatedly than he had to. Because he couldn't understand why so many Americans didn't see the evidence around them — that it's a lack of swift retribution (and the promise of a sequestered future) that encourages criminals to indulge themselves and take the plunge.

But then the study of history has fallen on hard times. So now we repeat the old mistakes on a scarier scale, out of wishful thinking and a misplaced faith in social engineering. Educated Americans and the modern mea culpa. Guilt-ridden because we're "privileged." Wandering in a wasteland of naiveté, blaming everything but the criminal for criminal behavior.

But there was nothing he could do about it. And getting irritated was a waste of time.

He picked up Pascal's Pensées and read until he felt like he had to move or he'd fall asleep. And then he got up and made himself a cup of coffee — right before the lights went off and the stereo stopped in the middle of Beethoven's Seventh.

Then the phone rang, which surprised him, because it usually went out before the electricity. He heard Walter Buchanan through a haze of static say it looked as though Journey was impacted. He was in a lot of pain, and Walt had already called the vet, but he probably wouldn't be able to get there, not with the roads the way they were.

Ben told Walter he'd be right out.

And then his phone went dead.

Horses can die of impaction, and they almost always die of a twisted gut, which has identical symptoms in the early stages. Nothing gets through their intestines, and they're in agony, and either way you have to keep them walking. But Walter shouldn't have to do that, not in this kind of weather. And anyway, Ben wanted to be with Journey. He wanted to talk to him and calm him down and be the one to make the decision if he had to be put down.

Ben had put on silk socks, two pairs of heavy wool socks, long underwear, his old wool Army pants, and two wool sweaters, as well as the fur-lined leather boots and hat (with ear flaps and face flaps) his sister had sent him from Alaska. He grabbed a wool scarf, and pulled on his heavy gloves, but he still stuffed his down mitts in the pockets of his old sheepskin coat — before he fought forty feet of storm to the garage.

He turned the key in the ignition of the old Plymouth, and congratulated his brother when it started.

He found a shovel and a bag of salt and tossed them in the back seat, along with jumper cables and a length of chain, since it was faster than fiddling with the broken lock on the trunk.

It was three above, according to the thermometer on the outside wall, when he closed the garage door. And the snowfall was so thick, and it was blowing so hard, he couldn't see ten feet in front of him.

He ought to stay home. He ought to just pull in the garage and go back inside before it was too late. Walter would figure it out, and he'd take care of Journey.

But Ben pushed in the clutch, shoved the car in reverse, and slid backward down the hill to the street.

He could normally get to Walter's in fifteen or twenty minutes, but it took more than an hour and a half just to get close to the old one-lane bridge that crossed the Moreton River at the end of the Buchanans' road. Most of the time, he could hardly see past the front of the car — just that swirling wall of white that became more blinding as the day grew darker. But at least there weren't any other cars to worry about. And once he crossed the river and got on Potter Road, there'd only be two more miles to Walter's.

Ben was wiping the inside of his windshield with a rag and praying wildly that he wouldn't run off the road again. He'd had to dig himself out four times because the drifting was so bad he usually couldn't tell where the road and the side began and ended. But there were still a few bare fields, scoured by the storm, where he'd seen corn stalks, close to the road, standing after the harvest — where the snow had been blown across them into drifts eight or ten feet high when the wind hit a hillside or a fence or a row of bushes.

Then finally, he was on the bridge. And at least he could tell where the sides were, with the old rusted railings, even with the frost on the inside of his windows. There was more ice under the snow here than on the roads, and he lost the Plymouth's rear end two or three times, but there were only a few more feet and he'd be off.

The next thing that happened was one of those unexpected events that come back to you in slow motion, if you live through them. One of those split-second reactions that get preserved in such clarity, the details pass by afterward, one by one.

There was a tree down in front of him, across the road. The branches, lying on their side, must have been fifteen feet high, and they were propping up the trunk so that it was lying on a slant, with the high end three or four feet off the ground. The tree had fallen on an angle too, and the left side of the road was completely blocked, so either he smashed into the trunk or he ran off the road on the right, where a low lying hill dropped down into a bank by the river.

He was trying not to hit the tree, and his car was flying off the road, off the right side, past the wall of snow that had grown on the hill — and then he was falling, sliding sideways down the bank, down toward the river, smashing hard into a huge drift, and shuddering to a stop.

Ben's head was against the steering wheel. And he had no idea how much time had passed. It was darker outside than he remembered. His head felt like it had been split open, and the taste of blood was in his mouth.

The car had stopped moving. And the engine wasn't running. And the world was filled with the roar of the wind and the whipping snow. He couldn't see where he was. He couldn't see anything out the windows except white.

The passenger side of the car was slanted down, way down away from his side of the seat, and he thought he could hear the river down below on that same side.

He imagined the car rolling over and over, landing in the ice and water. But then he forced himself to stop.

The driver's door was now above him at a disconcerting angle. And as he tried to reach for the handle, he was paralyzed by a savage shooting pain in his left shoulder.

He had muscle damage in that arm from the war, but he'd also separated his shoulder playing high school football, and that's more what this felt like. Any movement of his arm, especially forward or out to the side, was excruciating. And he had to use both hands to turn the handle.

But even then the door wouldn't budge.

When Ben leaned down the incline toward the passenger door, he felt the big, beetle-shaped Plymouth shift sickeningly, before it fell back into its original position when he pushed himself up into the driver's seat.

He was sweating now, even in the cold, and his jaws were clamped together. Battle anxiety. After sixteen years. He even had the same taste in his mouth. Animal instinct in the face of death.

He wiped blood away from his right eye, and then tried to lower his side window with his right hand, but the pressure of the snowbank made it impossible. It didn't look as dense against the passenger window, but all he could see through the windshield was a solid white wall of packed snow pressed against the glass. With the hill on his side, and the incline toward the river the way it was, the passenger side probably wasn't as tightly packed in the drift. But he couldn't get to it without unbalancing the car.

When he looked out the back window, he saw the faint red smudge of his own taillights reflected in the falling snow. He thought about leaving them on to attract attention, but decided it made more sense to save the battery.

It was a two-door sedan, and the rear side windows were too small to get through even if they weren't packed against the snow as solidly as the front. So he'd have to smash the rear window and climb out across the trunk.

He remembered the shovel he'd thrown in the back seat. But when he twisted toward the passenger side, he could feel the car slide. And he snaked back around, swiveling to the left, slowly, holding his breath, working himself up against the roof, until he was kneeling and facing the back. He took his coat and sweaters off, so he could squeeze over the top of the seat.

And then he was coiled in the back seat on

the driver's side, with a white-hot misery in his shoulder.

He had to stay on the driver's side too. And he wasn't at all sure he could get through that window without moving too far down the incline and flipping the car into the river.

Every movement he made made the car tremble. But it wouldn't do any good to think about it. Much better to mumble an abject prayer to the God of numbered hairs and concentrate on sliding the shovel across the seat and smashing the glass out against the wind.

When all that was left were a few curved shards sticking out from the metal frame, he looked at the size of that window and wished he was a very small man for the first time in his life. He laid the suede side of his sheepskin coat down on the bottom of the window, across the crushed-glass surface of the trunk, and put one of his sweaters back on for protection, before tossing the other out in the snow.

When he pushed himself through the oval ring, it felt like he was stripping off his own skin, bruising his shoulders and his chest and his pelvis, while tearing the tissue inside his shoulder.

Then he was sliding down the trunk of his car, panting and bloody and covered with rapidly cooling sweat.

The snowfall was so thick, even sheltered as he was by the rise above him, he could barely make out the river fifteen or twenty feet below.

But the angle of his car, when he turned and looked at it, hanging above the water, made him shudder. Because if the front end hadn't been wedged as deeply as it was in that hard-packed drift, he would've slithered down the bank and been sucked under an icy river. Although this wasn't the time to dwell on it. He had to decide what to do next, while he put on his coat and his down mitts and wrapped his scarf around his face.

Night had come down on him, and it must have been zero or below. There were no headlights now either to help him find his way, only the flashlight in his pocket and the wind on his right to give him a sense of direction.

He climbed the hill on all fours (which wrenched his shoulder even more) and discovered how much the drifted incline had sheltered him, when he took the fury of the storm straight in the face. A face that was already cut and stinging and probably beginning to swell.

Ben knew he ought to head straight toward Walt's. The cold was almost overpowering, and his face and feet and hands were already beginning to ache.

But he put his head down and leaned into the wind and worked his way over to the fallen tree.

It was maybe a foot and a half in diameter, where the saw had taken it down. The stump sat twelve or fifteen feet from the bridge, and he could still smell traces of bar oil. He could tell by the surface cuts too that it had been a chain saw, even though the chips and sawdust had already been covered over.

He studied the ground, but there wasn't anything left to see. The wind was cleaning that side of the road, wiping away the signs of human interference, while laying down a blanket of heavy snow.

Ben tried to evaluate what the tree lines and the terrain were like on his side of the river. And then he waded back across the bridge to the other side, into a cluster of evergreen trees where the road turned onto the bridge.

That's where the car had been. The tall spruce and fir grew into each other's sides and sheltered a small glade. The tire tracks were smooth ribbons, in the pale circle from Ben's flashlight, being filled by snow filtering down from between the trees. There was only a two-foot stretch left, but the tracks were distinct enough to tell him how deliberately he'd been set up.

Ben turned toward Walter's and put his face down, trying to keep his mind off his body and let his anger wrestle with the cold.

In '55, that snowplow driver had lost his way and frozen to death a hundred yards from a house he couldn't see. It wasn't any colder then, and the snow wasn't any thicker than it was now. The chances of anyone driving by were so small as to be nonexistent. And there weren't any houses anywhere near. Just Walt's farm and his sister's place, half a mile past his.

And yet Ben wasn't as afraid of death in the midst of that blizzard as a lot of people would have been. Not with his view of the universe. Its purposefulness. And its mercy. And not with Jessie gone. He'd seen too much death anyway. The novelty had worn off. Even though freezing to death would not be his first choice.

It had to be somebody who knew the land, and knew where he kept Journey, and understood about horses, as well as how to make trees fall in one direction rather than another. Ben wondered if the man had called him on the phone and then took the tree down (because if he had, he probably hadn't been gone long), or whether he'd done it in reverse. The tire tracks looked recent, but how could he have gotten to the bridge faster than Ben if he'd come from town?

He could've come from another direction. And speculation was a waste of time. Either way, he couldn't make this look accidental, not with the chain saw. Even though there wasn't much you could use to identify him. Just the marks left behind by the blade.

There have been murderers for whom Ben felt sympathy, but this person wasn't one of them. He was a coward and a cad. He watched Richard. He stood by and watched Grace. If the weather hadn't been so awful, he probably would've wanted to stay and watch Ben die. And if the incline had been steeper, or Ben hadn't brought the shovel, he might've been able to. Nothing swift and direct like a bullet or a blunt instrument in the back of the brain.

No, this guy doesn't want to get his hands dirty.

And it wasn't over either. Ben still had two miles to walk in sub-zero weather and forty-five-mile-an-hour winds.

And that wind cut and ripped and worked against the will. Ben's face felt like his fingers had when he was little, when they'd gotten stuck to a piece of ice and his mother had to pull them off. Which made Ben pull his scarf up for the hundredth time, and think about things besides discomfort.

Like the fact that it wasn't any worse. That he hadn't been badly hurt, or killed like he could've been, when the car flew off the road. And that he also had the boots and the hat and the goose-down mitts. Because without them, he probably wouldn't have had a chance of getting to Walter's place whole. So he'd already been spared, in reality. And he told himself to concentrate on that.

He thought about England next. The soft, rolling beauty of the Cotswold Hills in summer. The small stone cottages tucked in the turns and twists of ancient roads. The lush green grassland, salted with sheep. The western lochs and the highlands of Scotland, with their wild Caledonian forests.

At least it was a good thing his background was what it was, and he'd spent that summer cutting trees for the park service. It had occurred to him years ago that if you compared the cuts from more than one kind of chain saw, you could identify them like you could typewriter type, or cigarette ash, or handwriting. Certainly if they were different sizes and different makes. An eighteen-inch McCulloch and a thirty-six-inch Stihl wouldn't be a problem with the naked eye, although two of the same model would probably require magnification.

He wiggled his toes and moved his arms, even though it was difficult with his shoulder joint grinding against itself.

And he told himself not to think about it. He'd lived through worse than this. He made himself remember how cold it was being flown into France, hanging underneath that Piper Cub.

One foot. And then the other. Through two feet of snow, or three feet of snow, and sometimes a great deal more.

Not that Ben was complaining. There are worse things than drifts.

And one of them was coming up fast.

It was the woods on Ben's right, close to the edge of the road, that was making the snow blow into deep drifts. But once he got past those woods, and a not very long fence row of trees and bushes, the land would open into flat fields, and there'd be no more landmarks of any kind.

There'd be nothing to keep him on the road or aim him in the right direction. There'd be no reason not to wander off into nothing. There'd only be the wind, blowing in his face out of the west, to give him a sense of direction. And the wind can change and be deceptive.

I ought to put a compass on my key ring when I get home. Assuming, of course, that I actually do.

And I ought to write a monograph too. "The Process of Chip Formation in Relation to the Geometry of Chain Saw Cuts." Yeah, but who would read it? Chester? Only if he were investigating a chain saw murder. Wonderful. Very funny.

There's also more than one way to kill a man with a chain saw.

He was still floundering through deep drifts, but he was coming to the end of them. The woods had already thinned into a line of trees and brambles eight or ten feet away.

Ben tried his flashlight, but all it did was show him a swirl of white needles, and the relentlessness of the onslaught, shooting straight into him.

At least he knew he was going in the right direction — while he thought about what to do when the trees were gone. When it was just blackness and stinging snow.

He stopped to clap his hands together and stamp his feet and pull the frozen scarf up one more time.

And that's when he remembered the drainage ditches, the two or three isolated stretches on the left side of Potter Road. If he could figure out where they were, they could give him a sense of direction. But if he stumbled into one, he'd be colder and wetter and tireder when he got out.

The wind was battering against him, as though it would blow him over if he'd slowed his pace at all.

And it kept getting harder to make himself pick up his feet.

When did Mabillon set out the fundamental principles of the science of verifying documents, and what was the name of his book?

It was called *De re diplomatica.* And it was published in 1680. No, 1681.

The Museum of Mankind in the Burlington area of London has the most beautiful collection of South Seas materials in the world. Aside from the Bishop Museum in Honolulu. Royal Hawaiian feather cloaks in particular.

And what about John Wesley? He wouldn't have been the man he was without a winter gale. If he hadn't seen the Moravians on the verge of death, praying the way they did during that storm crossing the Atlantic, he might not have become what he was.

There's still more to do with that Moravian influence when I get back to Oxford. I probably ought to go to Woolwich again too.

And what was the name of that Methodist missionary who wrote *Life Among the Indians*? His letters still need to be annotated. Findlay? No. His first mission was in Sandusky. Finley. That was it.

And what was the name of John Whyte's daughter? The first white child born in the new world? Virginia something. Virginia Dare.

That's if you assume the Vikings didn't have children born here on their voyages to the New World.

A passage from Richard's journal came back to him, the part where Richard talked about walking with Bill Taylor in Indiana and evaluated Bill's work. And Ben began to think about common denominators.

Is there one, between the last journal and the notebook for the novel?

Yes. The life of a graduate student. I saw that when I first read them. Graduate school as Richard experienced it, interrupted and altered by the war, as well as how he'd planned it in his own fictive world.

Whatever happened to Roger Jones? The other roommate of Richard's, the one who'd survived the South Pacific? I haven't thought about Roger in years.

And where did David Krause go when he left I.U.? It would've been a shame if he hadn't gone back to school. He would've been a great student, if he'd ever gotten serious.

It was all worth thinking about. Indiana University at Bloomington. Led right to Alderton. And at least Ben knew what direction he'd have to take to look into it.

It was the viciousness of the cold and the stinging of the snow that Ben struggled against as he stumbled time after time. The immense weight of his feet, growing with each step, as well as the increasing preposterousness of making himself move.

There were no landmarks now. There hadn't been for some time. There was just the overwhelming cold. The stinging snow. The force of the wailing wind. The pain in his left shoulder. The aching cold in his hands and his feet and his face.

In some sense, ironically, the storm seemed, after a while, to take him in like an old friend. Perhaps because it was the snow he'd packed in his wounds near Trier that had helped keep him from bleeding to death then. And that the cleanness and the whiteness of the world around him brought back the sense he'd had there of being snatched by God from the jaws of death.

Though there was little comfort in any connotation connected with snow twenty minutes later. The one consoling reality he'd been counting on was taken away when the solid world under his frozen feet collapsed, and he was sucked into a snow-filled ditch.

He was buried up to his waist. And his torn shoulder had been ripped again, and all he could do was cradle that arm against his body with his other hand, while he battled the waves of pain.

Then he concentrated on his breathing, almost the way Jessie had when she'd had the baby, as he gathered himself for the effort of getting out. He'd have to pull himself up with his arms, and postponing that had a certain appeal.

On the other hand, there was water in the ditch, a foot maybe, in the bottom. He could feel it seeping into his boots as he struggled up onto the edge of what must have been the road, dragging himself out with his arms through shifting snow. Just like in Germany in '44.

The sub-zero air was searing the inside of his lungs, as he groaned and flailed and felt his arm tearing away from his shoulder.

But finally he was on his stomach on hard ground, with his arms curled under his chest. He lay there, trying to get his breath.

Trying to make himself want to move. Talking to God without using any words.

It'd be easy to lie there. To relax and let go. To curl up and fall asleep and be covered with a blanket of snow. He'd feel warm too as hypothermia progressed. A lot of people take their clothes off just before they die of cold.

He was trying not to remember what frost-bitten skin looks like, and what the treatment often is — when he thought for one split second, as the snow swirled in front of him, blown toward the ground and then whipped up again, that he'd seen a faint flickering pinpoint of light, far off on his right side.

He rolled over on that side and then knelt for a minute, before he dragged himself up onto his feet.

And then he put one foot in front of the other again. Just like he had before. That glimpse was enough to keep him going, with moments of false hope and flashes of despair, until he realized it was Walter's barn ahead and the lights were still on.

Still, it felt like years before he was edging his way around the wall of that barn, holding onto it with his hands, feeling his way to the other side, and pushing against the door.

"Ben! Is that you? What the devil are you

doing here! You all right?"

He was leaning against the inside wall telling himself to close the door. But he didn't seem to be able to make himself move his arms.

Walt pushed him out of the way, and slid the heavy wooden door sideways in its tracks. "What happened? There's blood all over your face!"

"How's Journey?"

"He's fine. Why? I just came out to break the ice on his water and stack some hay against the cracks in the west wall."

"You didn't call. Right?" Ben was sitting on a bale of hay, staring at the icicles on Journey's eyelashes.

"No! Why would I? Anyway, the phone lines have been out since two o'clock. We never lost electricity here, but my folks did over to Weston Road. How'd you get here?"

"I walked. From the river." Ben wanted to laugh at the expression on Walt's face, but he couldn't.

He just let Walter lead him to the house, with his good hand on the clothesline for direction, and Walt's arms around his ribs to keep him on his feet.

CHAPTER NINE

Sunday, November 27
Ben woke up under a down comforter, aching in every muscle and joint and tendon. His shoulder felt just like he'd thought it would, and yet it was a gift, under the circumstances, to be able to feel anything.

Walter's wife, June, was a nurse, and she'd patched Ben up and thawed him out the way you're supposed to with the beginnings of frostbite. His feet and hands and face would have to be protected from the cold for a while, and he'd have to put ice on his shoulder for the next few days. But it wasn't separated. Just torn and bruised. And he could live with that. Easily, all things considered.

It took him three tries before he could sit up and get out of bed. He stretched painfully and made himself move around, and then he stood in the shower and let hot water roll over him for a long time.

The snow didn't completely stop until late morning, but the plows had been out for several hours once the wind had died down and the drifting had slowed. And about one,

Walt got his chain saw ready and drove Ben over in a pickup truck with a snowplow blade.

They cut a slice off the stump as well as the trunk of the fallen tree. Then they initialed the sides that had the original cuts and put the cross sections in the truck.

Walter cut up the rest, because of Ben's shoulder, but Ben helped drag it off the road with his good arm. And then they went back to the house to get warm.

Walter loaned Ben his pickup, and when he started back to town about four, the weather was beautiful. It was hard to believe how much it had changed in one day. The temperature was up to fifteen, the wind was gone, and the drifts were still and serene, folding over each other like soft feather covers, curling where the pale sun warmed them, flashing where it touched the slick skin on top of the snow.

The country roads were still bad, and Ben had to plow himself out a few times, but the county plows had been able to keep the center of the roads clear as he got near Hillsdale, even though there were still cars buried where they'd been parked along the city streets.

Ben's house seemed all right when he got

home. He walked around it before he went in, but there weren't any footprints and nothing looked like it had been disturbed.

It was freezing inside. Most of Jessie's plants had been killed, but the water pipes were working. They were all in the center of the house and he'd insulated them when he'd renovated.

He got the Franklin stove roaring, and then relit the furnace and the water heater and tried the phone.

He started a fire in his bedroom fireplace, then got dinner out of the way. And once the chill was off, he took the box of Richard's papers out of the bedroom closet and sat down in the rocker with his feet toward the fire.

He started with the phone bills from September, listing all the long-distance calls Richard had placed. He cross-referenced those with Richard's address book, establishing that he'd called his aunt in Chicago, as well as three close friends he'd taught with in previous positions.

There were five calls unaccounted for in late October and early November — two to a number in Michigan, one to somewhere in Florida, another to a number in Indiana, and one last one to Columbus, a little after six the night Richard died.

Ben's phone rang while he was checking area codes, and it was Maggie, wondering how he was. She'd been trying to get him since early morning and it was only now that the phone would ring.

As soon as he finished with her, Ben called Richard's aunt in Chicago and his friends across the country. But none of them shed any light on what had happened to Richard.

He called whoever it was Richard had called in Michigan next. But he didn't get an answer.

And then his phone rang again.

It was Waldo Hubbard. He'd been trying to reach Ben since the night before, because he'd remembered something else about the day Richard died. It was right after Waldo had said good-bye to Richard outside his office at Ohio State. A member of Waldo's department (who'd just joined the staff that September), a young man by the name of Dr. David Krause, had run up to Waldo in the hall. David had seen Richard at a distance, and thought he reminded him of a professor he'd had years earlier in Indiana. Waldo had told David Richard's name, and David had said something like, "That's who I thought it was!" and rushed down the hall, down the same stairs Richard had taken.

Ben asked if David had seemed glad to see

him or hostile, and got the "hostile" answer he'd expected. He wrote down David's address and phone number, and then asked if Waldo had told Richard that David was teaching at Ohio State. Waldo was sure he hadn't. And Ben thanked him several times before he hung up.

He compared the Columbus number on Richard's phone bill with David Krause's home number, and then smiled to himself, as he rubbed the cleft in his chin.

David Krause. The man who'd held a grudge against Richard at I.U. had dropped out of the sky, after twenty years, the day Richard died.

He tracked Richard down and talked to him too. Or Richard couldn't have called him.

And I wonder why he did call him so soon. If he saw him that afternoon. Krause hated him at Indiana, that was obvious.

But that was twenty years ago, and you'd think he'd have gotten over it.

Somebody named David called my house and asked where I keep my horse. And Maggie gave whoever it was Walter's address and phone number, two or three days before the blizzard.

So is it a coincidence? Or did David Krause hear Richard talk to me in England and decide I knew too much?

Yeah, but if it was Krause who called Maggie, and he was up to no good, why would he give her his real name?

Ben ruffled his hands through his hair, and then stood up and stretched, while he thought about what to do next.

He tried the number in Florida first. But nobody answered.

Then he dug out his map of Columbus.

David lived on the southwest side, so it probably wouldn't take more than an hour. It was only seven-thirty anyway, so he ought to be able to get there and back and still follow up on the other calls.

He dialed Krause's home number. And then hung up as soon as David answered.

A little over an hour later, Ben was holding a child's red rubber boot, while smiling through a glass door at a small blond boy in blue-knit pajamas with built-in feet, who had to reach way up to turn the knob.

The boy looked like he was probably two and a half or three, and he was sucking his thumb through lips covered with peanut butter.

Ben smiled again.

And this time the boy smiled back. Like he was a happy kid who couldn't help it, even if it made him feel shy.

"I found this boot by the front walk. It almost looks like it might fit you." Ben laid it on the mat inside the front door.

But the boy just stared at the spoonful of peanut butter he was circling like an airplane above his head.

"Is your daddy home?"

"Yes." He said it very quietly and then started twisting the doorknob back and forth with his left hand.

"Would you tell him that a friend of his would like to talk to him?"

He nodded, but he didn't stop turning the knob. He was watching the brass catch slide in and out on the edge of the door.

"Maybe we ought to close the door, do you think? It's awfully cold outside."

The boy didn't answer. He just turned around and ran past the stairs toward the back of the house.

Ben waited, his fur-lined boots dripping on the hall rug. But nothing happened. He could hear a TV somewhere in the back, and there were kids laughing. Several, from the sound of it.

And he called David's name.

No one answered.

So he walked back through the hall to the kitchen.

There was a family room next to it, and

David was there, watching "Bonanza" with his wife and three small kids, two of them girls in pigtails.

"David?"

"Who the heck are you!" He was on his feet before he finished the sentence.

"I'm sorry to just walk in —"

"You oughtta be! Who do you think you are?" His hackles were up and his voice was outraged.

"Your boy answered the door, and I waited for quite a while. Anyway, I thought maybe you'd remember me. I'm Ben Reese."

"Ben?" David was as tall as Ben, but stockier, and he was walking toward him with a disconcerted expression on his broad, bearded face. "What are you doing here? Especially in weather like this?"

"I need to talk to you."

"What about?" He was scratching the right side of his beard and pointedly studying Ben.

"It's kind of a long story."

"Oh? Then we better go into the den. I guess." His tone of voice wasn't hostile, exactly. It was cool and careful and a little edgy, as he stared at Ben before he walked past. "What happened to your face?"

"I was in a car accident yesterday."

"What were you doing out on the roads?"

"Making a fool of myself, mostly."

"Yeah, right. You never did much in the old days without a darn good reason. So what's this all about?"

"Richard West."

"I should've known, right? I suppose he told you I was vicious and vitriolic and he couldn't understand why I'd talk to him like that!"

"No, he never mentioned it."

"That doesn't sound like our illustrious Professor West." David had led Ben into a small, book-lined room by the front door, where he'd just dropped into an office chair behind a desk made from orange crates and a hollow-core door. "At least not the Richard West I knew."

Ben was sitting on the edge of a brown corduroy couch, keeping his arm quiet against his ribs, while he gazed at David Krause. "Richard died that night. Not too long after he talked to you."

"Oh?"

"You knew?"

"Yeah. Waldo told me Monday. But if you're waiting for me to act like I'm sorry, you've got a long wait."

"You never faked anything when I knew

you before, so I guess I wasn't expecting you to start now."

"Do you like hypocrisy better?"

"No. Not at all. But there was never any doubt that you hated his guts."

"I had reason to hate him! You know that. You were there."

"Yeah, I was there. And I thought there were two sides."

"You would. You were one of his favorite protégés."

"I don't see it that way. But I can understand why somebody would. Anyway, after you saw him by Waldo's office, did you catch him in the parking lot?"

"No, he got to his car before I could stop him, so I followed him out to the zoo. You know what he was doing when I finally found him?" He paused for dramatic effect, his feet up on a file box and his thick-muscled arms crossed across his stomach. "He was lecturing a parrot on his grammar! Yeah, I'm not kidding you. And then he tried to make him say 'Ludwig von Beethoven.' Is that perfect or what? A parrot! That's the kind of student Richard always wanted."

"I don't know. I think Richard enjoyed hearing different opinions."

"So that's why people who disagreed with

him never got A's?" David was sliding his thumb down one side of his beard and his fingers down the other, like he enjoyed the feel of smoothing it against the edge of his jaw.

"You remember Harold Friedman? He was a Marxist. He took three courses from Richard and got straight A's. But then, he worked his tail off."

"So it was my fault!" David had picked up an arrowhead from the collection on his desk and was sliding it back and forth from one hand to the other.

"I didn't say that. But either way, it was over with twenty years ago."

"That's easy for you to say. You aren't the one he flunked!"

"What did the two of you talk about Friday?"

"Not much. I just told him what I thought of him."

"That was worth following him to the zoo?"

"Yeah. I never talked to him face-to-face when it happened. And I wanted him to know I got my doctorate."

"I'm glad you did, by the way. I still remember your essay on the Indians of North Dakota."

"Really?"

"Yeah. Richard kept a copy. I found it when I was looking through his papers. So was that the only time you talked to him?"

"No. He called me that night before dinner. He beat around the bush for a while, but I think he was trying to tell me that he wished he'd spent time with me after my mother died. He also invited me to dinner. Time unspecified, of course, so he wouldn't actually have to do anything about it. Anyway, I think his conscience must have been bothering him."

"Probably. His was more developed than a lot of people's. Would you have gone?"

"No!" David looked away, out the doorway toward the front stairs. "I don't know. Maybe it would've been amusing."

"So that was all he said?" Ben was sliding a finger along a cut next to his nose and staring at the cold, black window, watching David sideways out the corner of his eye.

"He told me you were at Alderton too. And I asked him if you'd gotten a horse. I remember you used to want one when we were all at I.U."

"What'd he tell you?"

"That you bought one a couple of years ago."

"He tell you where I keep it?"

"No. But I think it's time you told me

255

what this is all about."

"Richard was murdered. And a woman he talked to that night, right after he called you, has been murdered since. I talked to him that same night from England, and I was almost killed yesterday."

"You think I'm in danger because he called me that night!"

"No. But it's a very complicated explanation. You're from Minnesota, aren't you?"

"Yeah."

"You had a grandfather who had a farm?"

"No, an uncle."

"You used to help him cut firewood?"

"Yeah. What's that got to do with Richard's death?"

"What'd you do that Friday night, after you talked to him?"

"You accusing me of something?" David spit the words out, and his red-gold eyebrows burned in the desk light, even against his reddening face.

"No. I'm not accusing you of anything. I'm just tying up a few loose ends."

"Fine! I'll tell you what I was doing! Are you ready? I was sitting on a podium in front of a hundred and fifty people, introducing a friend of mine from the University of Wisconsin who was speaking to the Ohio Society of Anthropologists." David Krause laughed and stood up, reaching for a legal pad on a shelf above the desk. "The chairman of my department was there, so maybe you'd like his name and number. Here, let me write it down for you. His home phone's unlisted, so I can't give you that, but you can call him at the department of anthropology tomorrow." He'd picked up a ballpoint pen, and he was writing fast, slashing at the pad with his left hand. "Waldo wasn't there, or you could've called him. But I can give you a couple of other names too. No trouble at all."

"What time was the lecture over?"

"Nine-thirty or ten maybe."

"So when did you get home?"

"You got your nerve, Reese!"

"I'm not accusing you of anything." Ben rubbed his shoulder while he spoke, and then glanced at a paper he'd found in his coat pocket, making himself look as relaxed as he could, to help defuse David Krause. "I'm just checking out everything I can think of."

"So you're here because I hated Richard twenty years ago?"

"Wouldn't you consider it, if you were me? I was there when you threw the rocks through his window. I read a couple of the notes you wrote him too, back in Bloomington. And Friday's the day you came back into his life."

"Alright. OK. I can see that. But why you and not the police?"

"It's a long, involved story, believe me, but I'm helping the Hillsdale police."

"Can I substantiate that?"

"Sure. Ask for Chester Hansen. He's the chief of police. I can give you his home phone, if he's not in his office."

"Then I guess I'll take your word for it."

"So what time did you get home Friday night?"

"Right around three. Maybe a few minutes after. Fred Krueger and I, he's the speaker I told you about, we went out after the meeting and had a few drinks. We went to graduate school together, and we hadn't seen each other in four or five years. I'll give you his number too, if that'll make you feel any better."

"Thanks." Ben folded the paper and put it in the pocket of his sheepskin coat. "You didn't call me the day before Thanksgiving did you, and ask where I kept my horse?"

"No. Why would I do that?"

"That's another complicated story. But anyway, thanks, David. I appreciate the help."

"Yeah."

"What'd you do for Thanksgiving?"

"We drove to Cleveland in the morning,

spent the night with my wife's family, and then came home on Friday."

"At least you missed the blizzard. Your little boy's a good kid."

"Most of the time, yeah. You got kids?"

"No."

They were in the hall, headed toward the front door.

"You married?"

"I was. My wife died."

"That's got to be awful. What'd she die of?"

"Having a baby."

"Geeze."

"Thanks for the help, David."

"So you don't think I'm in danger?"

Ben had his hand on the front doorknob, when he turned and looked at David. "No, I don't."

"You know, it's funny. I was hopping mad when I talked to Richard West. I mean, I really let him have it. And he *took* it. He defended himself, yeah, but . . . I don't know. He seemed different to me. Than I remember. It almost looked like I got to him, like I —"

"Hurt his feelings? You probably did. Richard really meant well. He was actually a gentle person, if you can believe it. Even when he was oblivious."

"Gentle!"

"Inside. In his own way. Vulnerable too. You know what I mean? His mother died when he was six or seven."

"Did she? Then why didn't he understand what I was going through?"

"It was a complex situation. There were other issues besides what happened after your mother died."

"I don't see what's so complex about it."

"No?"

"But you know, once I yelled at him . . . I don't know . . . it didn't feel as good as I thought it would."

"It never does, does it? Thanks, David."

"Yeah. Let me know, OK? What you find out?"

"OK."

He's not going to lie about the lecture, so it's gotta be after that. Ben had laid three small pine logs on top of a layer of kindling in his bedroom fireplace, and he was shoving paper under the metal grate. Then it all comes down to the friend, Dr. Frederick Krueger. Whose phone, unfortunately, is out of order. It must've been quite a storm to shut down the city of Madison. Small flames were starting from the embers, curling back slowly through the smoking paper. So all I can do is try him again in the morning. After I call David's department chairman.

Krueger may lie, so I'll have to check out the details — the hotel people and the bartender. But do I believe David?

Yeah, I do.

I can't see Sarie or French being able to take down the tree. Neither of them looks strong enough to even handle a chain saw. And I know French is very proud of the fact that he was born and bred in a city.

I thought I put the phone bill with the Florida number back in the middle of the desk.

It was there under a legal pad.

And it turned out to be Bill Taylor's parents' home in Tampa.

Ben explained about Richard's death and why he was calling, and Mrs. Taylor told him that Richard had gotten in touch to tell them he was considering rewriting the draft of Bill's dissertation and having it published posthumously in Bill's honor. He wanted to find out what had happened to it, and he wanted to get their permission.

She'd told Richard that they'd kept it, but she wouldn't be able to get it to him till spring, because it was up at their house in Wisconsin in the attic somewhere. She'd never read it herself; she didn't understand those things. But she hadn't wanted to throw it away. Richard had asked something else about it too, but she couldn't quite remember what.

She said she'd call him back if it came to her. And Ben thanked her for her help.

Bill Taylor's dissertation.

That could be Richard's other "enterprise."

Yes, the light may be beginning to dawn.

Ben couldn't remember the title, but it examined the life of the minister who'd had dinner with George Washington the night before the Battle of Trenton and Germantown. Bill had discovered a diary fragment in which this minister had described the battle with unusual accuracy and insight. What was his name? He became president of Harvard after the Revolution. Timothy something. Timothy what?

Richard had had a copy, because Bill had gotten him to critique it for him before they enlisted. A carbon copy with coffee rings on it and Richard's handwritten notes in the margins.

So did he call Mrs. Taylor to find out what had happened to the original? Or was Richard looking for his own copy?

The phone rang, and it sounded louder than usual in that high white room, because

Ben was off in another time and another place.

When he answered, the person on the other end hung up. And Ben stared speculatively at the receiver. It might've been a wrong number. Or it could've been someone doing what he'd done when he called David — finding out whether or not he was home.

It was worth pondering when he had a minute, considering recent events.

But right then he was trying to re-create the January that Bill and Richard had enlisted. The packing and the furniture shuffling and the confusion.

He tried the Michigan number again too, as well as the one in Indiana, but didn't get an answer at either place.

He rubbed his right eyebrow and the side of his jaw as he looked out the window at the empty street. He stretched his good shoulder forward and backward, and put more wood on the fire.

And then he walked into his closet and took his British Webley sidearm down off the high shelf. He took it out of the shoe box and unwound the oiled cloth he kept it in. He released the catch and bent the dark blue barrel down, exposing the empty cylinder. He shook a handful of .45s out of the small yellow and red box.

But he didn't load the cylinder. It was a gut decision that had nothing to do with brain. He just snapped the barrel back and wrapped the pistol up again and put the shoe box on the shelf between his British commando knife and his Colt .22.

He lay down on top of his comforter and watched the fire, while he contemplated the twistedness of the human soul.

It makes perfect sense, on a certain level. But why would someone that capable steal from anyone else? And yet it wouldn't be the first time someone who could do the work had stolen another's. Any more than it would be the last.

After a few more minutes of staring at a corner without seeing anything, he walked over to Jessie's desk carrying Richard's checkbooks and address book, and sat down in the director's chair with his eyes on the center drawer.

He took out his Camels and his ashtray and pulled a cigarette out of the pack.

But then he put it back and shut the drawer.

It was late. One o'clock probably. His neck ached and his eyes burned, but he'd gotten through November, after learning more about the last two years of Richard's finances than he'd ever wanted to know. The list was long, but the patterns had fallen into place. There was nothing exceptional. Nothing out of the ordinary. Richard had been a frugal man, and a quietly charitable one.

But on November 2d, Richard had written an eight-dollar check to University Microfilms in Ann Arbor, Michigan — the institution where Ph.D. dissertations are kept permanently on file if the institution where they're awarded considers them important enough to preserve for the public.

Ben tipped his chair back and smiled, tapping the top of his ballpoint pen right in the cleft of his chin, before he put the papers back in his closet and went to bed.

He woke up an hour later. Why, he wasn't sure. But he decided to get up and check out the house, and he started with the front windows.

There was a car parked up the street at the top of the hill, a block or so toward town. He couldn't see what kind or what color.

But he threw on his robe and went downstairs in the dark. All the doors and windows were locked the way he'd left them. And he couldn't see any footprints except his own in the snow.

He looked out his bedroom window again

and saw the car was still there. Which was odd, on his street. There weren't many houses, and they were set back from the road with big garages and long driveways, so almost nobody parked on the street.

He turned on a lamp, and then turned it off again a minute or two later. And when he looked out, in the dark, the car down the street had gone.

He got back into bed, but he set his alarm for three. It wouldn't hurt to get up every hour and take a look around.

CHAPTER TEN

Monday, November 28
Ben checked the number on Richard's phone bill and dialed shortly after nine. Yes. University Microfilms, just as he'd thought. But the woman on the other end didn't know anything about Richard West. And he gave her the date and number of the check, as well as the dates of the two phone calls Richard had placed. She said she'd check around and see if someone else remembered. Ben told her it was a police matter, and asked her to call him collect that night, if she couldn't get back to him before business hours were over.

He called the number in Bloomington, Indiana, again and got the history department at I.U. The secretary didn't recall talking to Richard West, and the only faculty member Ben could remember who was still there had gone to a conference at McGill and wouldn't be back till the following weekend. Ben thanked her and hung up.

He called David's department chairman and his friend at the University of Wisconsin. It took a while to connect with them, but they both corroborated David's story. As did the bartender from Krueger's hotel bar.

So Ben decided not to bother with the Krause family trip to Cleveland.

Instead, he spent the day passing time.

He called a garage about towing his car and was put on a waiting list. He talked to Walter about keeping the truck. He cleaned more dirt off the painting in the basement, and then took off a patch of varnish, only to decide he'd taken it down too far. He hammered the frames together and stretched two canvases, but he didn't feel like starting a painting of his own. He did leg exercises and lifted weights with his right arm. He finished the last Peter Wimsey novel and wished there was another, and then he cleaned the connections on his stereo equipment. He tried to work on the Finley papers and failed to concentrate. He played the acoustical guitar for the first time in months. And he kept his doors locked the whole time.

By late afternoon he was wandering around the house aimlessly watering what was left of the plants. Maggie usually did that, and Ben began to wonder if he was doing it right. But second-guessing himself made him even more impatient, and he overwatered a grape ivy half-deliberately.

An hour or so later, the phone rang, and Ben ran into the library to answer it.

It wasn't University Microfilms. It was Edward Campbell, who, after considerable dithering, asked Ben to serve on his dissertation committee. Ben wasn't sure he knew enough about Johnson to be able to contribute. So they discussed the dissertation, and when Ben could see it, and when the defense was to be, before he accepted and got off as fast as he could, to keep the phone free.

It was almost seven fifteen. He ought to fix himself something to eat. A salad, maybe, and some scrambled eggs.

He probably ought to call Chester, but he didn't want to. Not yet. Not until he had something more like proof than a half-theoretical supposition.

He thought about calling Ellen Winter to find out how her work was going, but that didn't make any sense. The phone would be tied up then too, and they already had a meeting scheduled for later in the week.

He finally went so far as to look at the pictures in Richard's cookbook, much to his own amazement.

But then the phone rang a few minutes before eight. It was a collect call from a woman at University Microfilms in Ann Arbor, Michigan, a Suzanne White.

On November 12th she had mailed Dr. Richard West a copy of a dissertation titled,

Reverend Timothy Flint: Early American Influence. And the name on the title page was the one Ben expected: James Theodore Cook, Ph.D.

He asked her to send him a copy, and began humming the hunting part from Vivaldi's *Four Seasons* without remembering what it was.

He sat down at his desk in the library and typed as fast as he could — with the old war injuries in his left hand — pausing ever so often to stare at the fireplace wall. He gathered his papers together and put them in a grocery bag, with the phone bills and the check book, and took it upstairs. He walked through his bedroom into the bathroom and put the bag in the laundry basket under the old free-standing sink, being careful to replace the top before sliding the basket back where it belonged.

Then he picked up the phone and dialed without looking up the number. "Mary Ann? . . . This is Ben Reese. Did you have a good trip? . . . I'll bet! Yeah, it was terrible here . . . So is your husband home? . . . Ah. Well, you know how it is. Once you get used to exercise on a set schedule, it's hard to make yourself stop . . . He spends time with the kids when he's home though doesn't he? . . . Yes . . . Well, I'll try to catch him over there . . . OK, thanks."

Ben held his finger on the button and stared at the phone. Then he dialed Chester's home and waited while his wife went to get him. "Hi, Chester . . . Did you? . . . No, I'm OK. Is it 9:30? . . . Yeah, my clock stopped and I wasn't sure my watch was right . . . I also wanted to tell you that I'm off on an errand, and if you don't hear back from me by midnight, the papers explaining who the murderer is are in a paper bag in my bedroom. You'll kind of have to look around, though . . . Thanks Chester, I'll talk to you later."

Ben held the receiver away from his ear and smiled before he set it down gently in its cradle. Chester had gone way out of his way for him and probably deserved better. But first he had to talk to Jim alone.

All the doors were locked except the janitor's door to the basement. There weren't any lights on in the pool wing when Ben went to look, but the main halls were lit. After checking the old basketball court on the first floor, Ben picked his way up the front stairs on his way to the men's dressing room.

He opened the first door and then the second one four feet past the first. And then he saw Jim, standing naked in front of him, pulling on the small shiny bathing suit he'd brought back from the Riviera.

"Ben! I thought you might put in an appearance."

"Since God took pity on me and I managed to survive."

"Are you alone?"

"Yeah, but I've talked to Chester. And I left the papers he'll need to prosecute where it'll take him long enough to find them that you and I should have a chance to talk."

"I see." Jim cocked his head to one side and gazed pointedly at Ben, before he shifted his glance to the door. "What a storm, huh? That was the worst blizzard I've seen since I was a kid. They got the roads cleared faster than I thought they would." Jim's things were distributed carefully on both benches; his comb and his towel and his terry cloth robe were on the one behind him, next to the bottle of shampoo he picked up and began pouring into a blue plastic squeeze bottle. "I find that if you dilute your shampoo and put it in a bottle with a narrow tip, it's much easier to apply. You should try it sometime." He was screwing the pointed applicator top on the hair-dye bottle he'd adapted for this purpose, smiling at Ben as though he were glad to see him. "What happened to your face?"

"I hit the steering wheel when the car landed. When did you cut down the tree? You couldn't have gotten there from town any faster than I did."

"I called you from Weston Corners and then cut the tree. You know where I mean, that crossroads south of the river, with the Texaco station and the carryout? It can't be more than a mile and a half from the bridge. I had the jeep from the grounds department too, and that made it easier. Except what I would've done if the pay phone had been out, I don't know."

"You left a lot more to chance than you did with the other two."

"Well, I couldn't see myself attacking you physically. Not with your experience. No, the real problem was that you don't have weaknesses. You don't drink to speak of, or take sleeping pills, and you don't have a heart condition. To tell you the truth, I thought I improvised rather well, considering I was in a rush. Mary Ann was due back yesterday. I could say I was home working, if she wasn't there to see I wasn't. That's one of the advantages of being president of a university. People don't expect you to lie, except in an official capacity, and then it's called alumni relations!"

"What were you planning to do last night?

Break in while I was asleep and turn on the gas in the stove?"

"Very good! I knew it wasn't foolproof, but time was running out."

"How could you do it, Jim?"

"Ah, but you don't know that I actually, technically, murdered anyone!"

"No? What would you call it?" Ben had taken a step toward him without noticing particularly.

And Jim backed away toward the lockers. "Now wait a minute, Ben. If you want to discuss this, you have to stay right where you are!" Jim was pale and thin, and he didn't look as muscular as some swimmers, even though he was tall and fit and well coordinated.

He reminded Ben of a hothouse plant that's been kept from the sun too long, or maybe a stalk of white asparagus that's cultivated underground. "Why are you so willing to talk about it? There's not as much concrete evidence as the rest of us might like. At least not at this stage of the investigation."

"Why!" Jim looked Ben straight in the eyes and then slipped his feet into his rubber sandals. "I think you know why already. Of course, I'd also like someone to see it from my perspective. You and I have known each other for twenty years. I thought you'd be able to empathize."

"How could you sit there and watch them die? I don't understand it. These were people you knew, not strangers on the street."

"That's sloppy reasoning on your part. Most murders take place within the family unit. You know, Ben, I'd feel a lot more comfortable if you'd sit down on that other bench. Assuming you still want to talk about this, and obviously you do."

Ben considered it, and then sat next to Jim's neatly folded pants and shirt. "You took his journals, and used my books as a blind, because you were afraid he'd written about you and the dissertation?"

"Of course."

"Is it OK if I take off my coat?" Jim nodded. And Ben laid his sheepskin coat down on the right side of the bench. "I bet you even waited, didn't you, after they were dead? Just to be sure they couldn't be resuscitated and embarrass you."

"Better safe than sorry, Ben, as our mothers used to say."

"But how could you look at Richard in that much pain and not do something to help! And what about Grace? That must've been pleasant, watching her make a mess of herself. How'd you get her to take the extra pills? Dissolve them in her drink, wash the glass afterwards, and then put it back in her hand?"

"She was a weak, silly, self-destructive woman, and she always took twice as many as she was supposed to. She'd taken two before I got there, and she remembered that, to begin with. She's the one who brought it up. She kept talking about her bereavement, and her nerves, and how she couldn't sleep without her medication. I told her she hadn't taken her pills, and gave them to her once. And then I dissolved three or four more in her drink. But that's not to say that I enjoyed it! What kind of person do you think I am? If Richard hadn't been trying to run everybody else's life, none of it would've had to happen!"

"You ready to tell me about Bill's dissertation?"

"I suppose. I won't talk about it with anyone but you." Jim sat down on the bench opposite Ben, in front of a row of lockers, absently moving his towel to the side, with his eyes on the signet ring he was twisting on his little finger.

And that's when Ben picked Jim's keys up from the bench and slipped them in the pocket of his corduroy jacket.

"Richard had decided to publish Bill's dissertation. 'In honor of Bill's memory and his rightful place in the historical community.' He'd had a carbon copy of it years ago, as I'm sure you know. But he couldn't find it, and he finally remembered that he'd given it back to Bill right before they enlisted —"

"And then he discovered that Bill's parents only had the original, and had never known there was a copy."

"Exactly. Well. You know what he was like!"

"Yes, I do."

"He knew I was having trouble with Valley Forge before he enlisted. So out of the blue, he asked me what topic I'd finally settled on for my dissertation. And that, of course, was the question I'd been dreading since the two of you came back from the war." Jim glanced at Ben, then looked down at the vinyl floor. "All these years I've been waking up in the middle of the night in a cold sweat, worrying that you and Richard would find out I'd used Bill's dissertation, and I'd be drummed out of academia."

"Wouldn't the word 'stolen' be more apt?"

"I suppose. If you insist."

"It never occurred to either of us. We were busy. And we didn't have any reason to think about our graduate work, once we'd finished our degrees. But why did you come here, if you were that afraid we'd find out?"

"There weren't any other universities beating on my door offering me a presidency, now were there?"

"And you had to be president of a university."

"Richard could have found out, exactly the same way, no matter where I was. But then, of course, after he'd asked me about my dissertation, he began hinting around, making his scathing asides —"

"And then he called you that Friday night and asked you to come to his office."

"Yes. He had a copy of my dissertation in the middle of his desk, and he looked at me like an avenging angel. His idea of an avenging angel, I hasten to point out."

"No doubt."

"I tried to explain to him what it was like for me, in graduate school. I was washing dishes, and teaching, and trying to do research too. I was so tired, Ben, I couldn't remember anything. I'd fall asleep in the library and wake up with someone tapping me on the shoulder, telling me not to drool on their irreplaceable tomes! If it had gone on much longer, I would've had a nervous breakdown, I really would have. Of course, you don't know what that's like, do you?" Jim's deep-set eyes turned on Ben, and the hatred and the hostility cut across years of posing and politeness. "Being afraid you'll humiliate yourself by exposing your weaknesses to the rest of the world? Not to mention the people you care about most!"

"I know what that's like. Everybody does."

"I'd met Mary Ann by then, and I wanted to marry her, but her father . . . well . . . he wouldn't have allowed the little princess to marry someone like me! He owned half of Bloomington, and what was I? A penniless nobody from a dilapidated dairy farm. Not without a Ph.D. I had to have it, Ben! Can't you understand that? You know what my prospects would have been in academia without one!"

"But you could've —"

"Of course, you don't know what those years were like. You were doing your duty, and I was home, hiding my flat feet under a desk! Richard thought I was thrilled and pretended not to be. But then he never was very compassionate, was he?

"It was right then, right when I was overworked and worried about losing Mary Ann, that he wrote and told me Bill was dead." Jim was staring at the wall across from him, with his hands hanging lifelessly between his knees. "I had to pack his things. They were still in his room in the old apartment. And I sat there and looked at the draft of his dissertation. I remember my palms were sweaty, and it was that onion skin paper and I kept smearing the ink from the typewriter ribbon." Jim was looking at Ben, but his eyes were empty.

It almost looked to Ben as though he was seeing himself, the way he was before he made that choice.

"Bill's advisor had left. I don't know why, now that I think about it. The other two on his committee had enlisted. And I'm not even sure what happened next. I just remember thinking that it didn't make any sense for all Bill's work to go to waste. You know, Ben, he was the only person there who ever really took the time to talk to me — to ask me what I thought and listen when I told him, take me along when he went places. Bill wouldn't have minded. He would've wanted to help. All I had to do was go to my advisor and tell him too much had already been done on Valley Forge, that I couldn't find a new angle on it, and I thought I'd approach the period from another tack.

"Then I spent another year pretending to write a dissertation while I polished his. The Flint diary excerpt Bill found in the library made all the difference. Here was a new perspective, the firsthand reaction of a knowledgeable source. I mean, that's what my life has been like! I worked my rear end off year after year, and he worked as a page one summer in the library and found a piece of Timothy Flint's diary stuffed in a book on Charlemagne!"

"Life isn't fair. Is it Jim?"

"Yes, well, Richard was less subtle, the last time I saw him. He said I blame everybody else for my own shortcomings and 'take life's little inconveniences as a personal affront.' But of course it was easy for him to pontificate. The rich Chicago doctor's son! Nothing's too good for precious little Dickie! Remember the food boxes at Christmas from Marshall Field's? My father hated my guts, and found a thousand ways to tell me that every day I spent on his stinking farm!"

"But you could've written a dissertation in your sleep. Why would you decide to steal Bill's?"

"There wasn't time for me to start over! I was in debt. And there was this other guy, a lawyer, who was interested in Mary Ann. If I didn't come up with something soon . . . well . . ."

"So the department accepted the dissertation?"

"My advisor knew nothing about Bill's work, and he was thrilled with it. He was imagining articles in journals under both our names. Flint's trip down the Hudson to the Battle of Trenton, his evaluation of Washington's character. Paul Harrison could hardly wait!

"But you know Richard. When a principle was involved, he was immovable. Nothing I said made any difference to him. None of the normal sorts of recompense would have tempted him. Well, can't you see what would have happened to me? 'President of university stripped of office, degrees, and reputation for plagiarizing the dissertation of a war hero!' Could you have lived with that? Don't say it, Ben! I know, you've lived through worse, and nobody who came back from the war has let any of us forget it!

"In any event, I knew *I* couldn't have stood it. James T. Cook, laughingstock! And neither was I willing to subject Mary Ann and the children to it either. Not Mary Ann. I couldn't have looked her in the face. It may come as a surprise, but she actually thinks I'm quite an exceptional person. But then her standards aren't as high as yours and Richard's.

"Anyway, I'm obviously too old to start

over in some other field. And who would give me the chance, after something like that? Yet there's one thing you have to understand, Ben. It wasn't premeditated. You hear me? I begged him, Ben! What good would it do Bill to bring it all out now? But that didn't move him, naturally. Not Richard! And I was desperate. I started yelling at him, telling him how I'd improved Bill's work, how Bill was never very bright, and he was too self-effacing to assert even his historical claims. And then Richard began to choke. He fell back in his chair and grabbed his chest, and then he took out his pills. I had a handkerchief in my pocket, and all I had to do was pull the bottle out of his hands. I didn't even have to watch. I just turned my back on him and waited."

Ben didn't say anything for a minute. He studied James Cook's face in silence. "You didn't just watch Richard, did you, Jim? You took the blue pillow off the wicker chair and smothered him with it."

"He died of a heart attack! You said so yourself!"

"He started having an attack, and you took the pills away from him, yes, but then you decided to hurry him along with the pillow. Didn't you? While he was helpless.

Then when it occurred to you that if he suffocated, the coroner would know he'd been murdered, you took the pillow away and watched him die, because you wanted it to look like natural causes."

"Chester never would've questioned it. But then you came back, didn't you, Ben, and you couldn't let it alone! If it hadn't been for you, Grace would still be alive!"

"You watched Grace too, didn't you? You saw her slip away. You saw her vomit and gag, and you heard all the sounds of human helplessness, and I bet you weren't even tempted to help her back. What's really ironic is that she didn't know anything anyway. So her death was a waste, even from your point of view."

"But she saw him that last night! She said he'd uncovered an act of pride and selfishness, which they together were going to 'expose to the world!'"

"She must've been embroidering by the time she talked to you. She told me that he said he'd 'uncovered an old injustice,' but he didn't explain what he meant. Although I find it interesting that you at least recognized the description of your own activities."

"That's a rather venomous remark, coming from you. Good old Ben Reese! He sees your weaknesses but he's much too polite to mention them to your face. It must be wonderful to be so superior! You and Richard. Always so smug! Always so sure you can describe the parameters of the universe! Knowing which fork to use, and where to buy your clothes! You never smelled like cow dung in civics class, did you!"

"I was just as poor as you were when I was a kid. What our families were like isn't even debatable. But Richard was right. You don't take responsibility for your own actions. You take the easy way out and blame everybody else. You just told me it was Richard's fault you had to kill him! Can't you see how that sounds to someone else? Jim Cook has to get what he wants, no matter who it hurts! Isn't that right?"

"I thought you'd at least try to be objective and understand what it was like for me. But oh no! You're just like Richard! Self-righteous and sanctimonious. Maybe some day you'll regret what you've made me do!"

"That's interesting. What *I've* made you do!" Ben smiled in disbelief and then shook his head as he stared at Jim. "I'll tell you one thing, I'm glad God has mercy on all our souls, mine as much as any, because it'll be a while before I'm able to forgive you the way I should."

"Shut up! Shut up, do you hear me! You

hypocrite!" Jim grabbed the squeeze bottle and lunged toward Ben, squirting shampoo in his eyes before Ben could stop him.

Ben was wiping his eyes with his bare hands when the lights went out, and he heard Jim say, "I'm putting an end to it now, Ben, and if you come after me, I'll either take you with me or I'll die trying!"

The hall door slapped open and shut while Ben stumbled against benches and rows of lockers, trying to remember where the sinks were in the other room. Then he was rinsing his eyes and grabbing a paper towel and groping his way toward the door.

He found the light switch to the dressing room between the two doors, but when he got out in the hall, it was pitch black. Ben didn't know the building well, and he had no idea where to turn on the lights.

He'd left the house without a flashlight, like an idiot.

And then he'd relaxed his guard, which was worse.

But he had Jim Cook's car keys, and Jim wasn't going anywhere without them, not in a bathing suit and sandals.

At least Ben had worn desert boots. It didn't make up for being taken by the shampoo, but crepe soles and silence were going to be important.

Something smashed down below him. It sounded like glass. Shattering and then scattering across something hard.

Ben waited, staring into the dark, listening.

Nothing.

Nothing else.

He had to move fast and clean — and he was. His senses were amplifying the world already, synthesizing and evaluating like they had in the war.

He slid his hands along the cold, smooth-plastered walls on his way toward the front stairs. His eyes burned, back inside their sockets, but he kept them open, reaching into the blackness in front of him.

The pain in his shoulder was gone.

Adrenaline did that almost instantly. There was only Ben's mind, straining in the dark, working off his senses.

Jim Cook knew his way around those halls. He swam in the gymnasium pool five nights a week. And he could come at Ben from anywhere.

Ben listened then, holding his breath. He could hear Jim somewhere down below. He could hear a rubber sandal slap against a foot.

And then he had the old metal banister in his hands.

Remember to count, and feel for the first step.

Then the next.

Then feel for a switch at the bottom.

It lit the hall he'd left on the floor above. And as soon as he'd turned it on, he turned it off. His own visibility put him in danger in the dark; like a prisoner of war, caught in the sweep of a searchlight.

He listened, leaning over the metal rail, his skin stretched tight over a network of straining nerves.

Follow the railing to the next set of stairs.

Thirteen, probably, like the last flight.

Feel for the edge with your toe, then step.

Then wait at the bottom by the front door.

There should have been an exit sign above it, but there wasn't. There was glass underfoot. Undoubtedly red. Crunching more loudly than Ben would've believed possible.

It was an old building that had been built as an armory and converted later, so there were very few windows anywhere and none in the front hall. There were just the two stairways to the second floor, one on either side of the double doors, with a hallway between them that led to the gym.

Ben stood with his back to those doors and listened.

He glided silently along the central pas-

sage with his right hand on the wall underneath the stairs, heading toward the archway
that led to the old gym.

There was a wide hall between the end of
that staircase and the gym itself, and he
crossed that fast.

He was touching the archway — his right
hand was on the side of it — and he stopped
and listened, losing even more time, if Jim
was going where he thought he was.

What other option did Jim have? Almost
barefoot and in his bathing suit, with the
temperature hanging near zero.

But he still had to get Ben out of the way.
And he'd want to choose the time and place.

Ben waited on the edge of the old basketball court, where gym classes now played
volleyball. It was all eerily quiet. And very
cold. He could feel the air stirring against his
face. And then he thought he heard someone
move across the floor.

Ben froze. Listening. Straining with his
stinging eyes against the dark.

He could feel the edge of a gym mat with
his right foot. He could smell stale sweat,
and musty towels, and old hemp climbing
ropes, somewhere off on his right. He could
hear a branch scratching across the painted-
over metal-frame windows high on the opposite wall. He could even see a graying in

the blackness across that painted glass, up near the two-story ceiling.

But no. There was nobody there.

And then, before Ben had a chance to turn, the hairs went up on the back of his neck. And he could feel someone behind him.

He'd heard something. A hand sliding on a door frame. Not a sandal, but maybe a bare foot on a wooden floor. A quick-smothered breath. Something.

And then he could smell Jim's after-shave. Strong and expensive and faintly cloying.

Ben swiveled silently toward the arch, working out the floor plan. The corridor in front of him with the basement stairs on either side; hallways on the left and the right; an alcove with a drinking fountain in one of them (the right, from what he could remember) and a wooden telephone booth in the other, both fairly close to the stairs; a pop machine too in the hall beside the fountain; and deep doorways down both corridors.

An uncomfortable number of hiding places, and Jim would know them all.

Ben shifted to the right, toward the center of the archway, to give himself more options. He held his breath and listened.

He could see and hear in ways he couldn't

have explained. Like a cat. Or a dog making midnight rounds. It's a physical phenomenon, documented in war and danger. And he inhaled silently in every direction.

He could smell the cologne. And he could smell the fear.

And he knew where Jim was.

The hall on the left. Close. In the phone booth probably. Behind some kind of obstruction.

Ben could feel the anger and the desolation and the panic. And he kept his eyes on that left-hand wall.

He had to get his bad shoulder out of the way, and he slid forward, quietly, turning counterclockwise, until his back was toward the stairs.

Ben could hear Jim breathing. He could hear the tightness and the desperation. And he knew it was dangerous, letting Jim know exactly where he was.

He didn't like doing it, but something inside him kept telling him to try again. "Jim, it doesn't have to be like this. You and I should be able to talk." Ben was ready to spring if he had to. His arms were balanced away from him and his legs were tensed and bent. "You know what I mean, that's why you explained it. And I do understand better than I did. All these years, you've been living in misery. Climbing the academic ladder and waiting for it to get kicked out from under you.

"But there's more to life, Jim. And there's more to death." Something moved, or seemed to. And Ben stopped breathing and listened. "Why not give yourself time to think about what you're doing? Doesn't that make sense? And to think about Mary Ann and the kids too?"

"I am thinking about them!"

Ben could feel it, and hear it, and smell the attack.

And he was ready for it.

What he didn't expect was the weapon.

He couldn't see it coming in time to stop it, but he kept it from shattering his head. He heard it thud against his ribs at the same instant he felt the blow from something very hard and heavy. An Indian club, as it turned out, which broke three ribs under his left arm.

Even so, as Jim swung the club back to hit him again, the side of Ben's right hand broke the bone under Jim's nose, exactly the way he'd intended it to. Jim screamed and fell against Ben, pushing him back, in his panic.

There may have been method in it too, because Jim had put a chain across the stairway (a cordon they used during volleyball games) and it hit Ben above the knees.

He went over backwards in the dark, smashing down the stairs, feeling the sharp metal edges in too many places, while he worked to protect his head.

He landed on his side on the last two steps. But he didn't stay there. He shoved his back up against the wall.

Everything else that hurt was overpowered by the pain in his ribs. Yet he forced himself to stand, still leaning against the wall, listening, sweat running down his neck and along his sides.

Jim was starting down the other stairs, and Ben crouched down and crept across, dropping beside the wall below the railing. There was an exit sign in the left-hand hall, and he could see most of the floor and the outline of the bottom steps.

Jim was inching his way down. Slowly. Tentatively. Trying to blow the blood out of his nose and wiping it on his arm. "I don't want to fight anymore, Ben. I mean it. Here, I'll throw down the club."

It landed at the bottom of the wall on the other side of the center hall and bounced a few feet to the left. "I've left two letters with my things upstairs — one for you, and another for Mary Ann. Let me go, Ben. Please. I can't stand to see her again!"

Ben tackled Jim as he stepped off the last

stair. He shoved him down on the floor, twisting his right arm behind him and grinding his own left knee into the middle of Jim's back, while he pulled Jim's thumb back as far as it would go without dislocating it.

"Ben, listen to me." He was talking between clenched teeth, gasping against the pain in his hand.

And Ben took pity on him and lightened the pressure on his thumb.

"I don't want to go to trial, Ben —"

"That doesn't come as a big surprise."

"But it's not the press and the publicity!"

"No? Why do I find that so hard to believe?"

"It's that I can't face Mary Ann and the kids again! I can't, Ben. Can't you understand that? I'm afraid of what I'll see in her eyes!" Jim laid the side of his face down on the cold terrazzo floor. And when he exhaled, it sounded like a strangled sigh. "I want her to be able to start over without me being a burden in some prison!" He was sobbing. The whole length of his body was shuddering under Ben's.

"I'm sorry about Mary Ann. But I can't let you go, Jimmy."

"I'm not asking you to let me go, just let me get to the pool!"

"Why didn't you? You could've gotten there before I could've stopped you."

"I tried, but there wasn't time! Please, Ben!"

"I can't."

"Why!"

"Because it's not up to me."

"Who then, Chester?"

"No. I think God has opinions about what we do, and those are the ones that matter."

"And you know exactly what your 'God' wants from me? Come on, Ben! Put yourself in my place!"

"I am, believe it or not. I'm actually trying to help you." Ben had begun pulling his own tie off with his left hand, and the pain almost took his breath away, but he never relaxed his grip on Jim's thumb.

"You're no better than I am! You hear me, Ben?"

"I hear you."

"How many Germans did *you* kill?"

"As many as I had to, to stay alive."

"So who are you to judge me!"

"I want you to listen to me very carefully. I'm about to tie your hands behind your back. If you don't cooperate *completely*, if you hassle me in *any way*, I *promise* you that I will make you hurt in places and in ways you never imagined possible! You got me? You understand? Answer me."

"Yes."

"Good. Now bring your left arm back behind you very, very slowly."

CHAPTER ELEVEN

Tuesday, November 29
"Not only did you have enough out-and-out gall to pretty much take over a police investigation, you withheld evidence!" Chester was walking back and forth in the middle of Ben's kitchen with his hat shoved back on his head, warming his hands on a mug of coffee.

"That's true." Ben had settled his elbow on the arm of his chair and was starting to adjust the sling on the back of his neck. "And I'm not sure how to explain it, either, so it'll make any sense to anyone else."

"You never should've gone after him alone! You knew he was desperate! That was completely unprofessional, and you knew it, with your background, and all and everything." Chester pulled a director's chair away from the table and sat down hard, tossing his hat on the counter by the sink. "But I tell ya, the worse part is that after I gave you all the information and help I had, you shoulda treated me better!"

"I know, Chester. I agree. But he was so obsessed with his reputation, I guess I wanted it to be the two of us first. I thought he'd be more likely to talk to me alone too. And I also wanted to hear what Richard's last minutes were like." Ben had his feet up on the empty chair, and he was stirring his coffee, watching the steam swirl in the air. "You wouldn't have gotten first degree murder. Right? You had to have a confession. If he talked to me first, it was more likely he'd talk to you, don't you think? And either way, I could testify."

"Yeah, if you lived!"

"It was also my own pride, I suppose. My own sense of chivalry. Mortal combat between two antagonists who've known each other as friends. But I didn't treat you very well. I don't know what came over me, really. I'm sorry, Chester."

"Yeah, you oughtta be!" Chester glared at Ben over the rim of his cup and then set it down in front of him and pushed the handle around in a circle. "You think he had the guts to drown himself?"

"He wrote the notes, and he was on his way to the pool. But whether he would've gone through with it I don't know." Ben rubbed the right side of his jaw, while he stared out the window across the fields.

"There're reporters coming in from all over like maggots crawling on a corpse, and you know they're gonna hear about you, there's no way they won't."

"But you can try to keep it quiet."

"Yeah, I can try. And Jim's getting cagier, since he talked to his lawyer. I mean, I've got his confession. And I got it after I'd read him his rights, thank God. But it sounded like he was backpedaling this mornin'. We've still got your testimony, plus the paper evidence you put together. There're the two notes he wrote too. And we've got the blue fibers on his overcoat. I told ya they match the ones the coroner picked out of Richard's mouth? Yeah, and the ones on his desk too. The boys are still comparing fibers from Grace's house to what's on Jim's clothes —"

"And you've got the slices from the tree trunk that match his chain saw."

"Right. So I'm not worried. I'd just have some kind of respect for him if he'd admit what he done and take his medicine like a man."

"Why do you think Craig French lied about being in his office that Friday night?"

"I think he's an ornery, uncooperative kind of guy, and he doesn't trust nobody, and he was trying to stay out of the investigation. He could've been worried about the murderer coming after him too. But you! You're too blasted independent for your own good. Chivalry! I can't believe you said that!"

"More coffee?"

"Thanks. Got any more milk?"

"Yeah, if you'll do me one more favor."

"You got yourself some nerve, boy."

"I know, but this isn't for me, really."

"Well? What is it this time!"

"Take him these books when you get a chance." Ben picked up *Perelandra* and *The Great Divorce* and pushed them across the table toward Chester. "Jim's not going to want to see me for a while."

"That's for sure. Who's C. S. Lewis?"

"He's a British writer who talks about Christianity in kind of unexpected ways."

"You think he'll read them?"

"I don't know."

"You're not feeling guilty, are ya?"

"No. But I meddled in his life. He probably wouldn't be where he is if it weren't for my interference, and that makes me responsible for him on some level. Anyway, aren't we supposed to be our brothers' keepers?"

"Maybe, but —"

There was a knock on the front door, and when Ben went to answer it, he found Ellen Winter standing on the porch looking like she felt ridiculous.

He brought her into the kitchen and

poured her a cup of coffee without thinking to ask if she wanted one.

"Hello, Mr. Hansen."

"Morning."

"I didn't mean to interrupt, Dr. Reese, but we had an appointment at nine. When you didn't show up, and I heard about Dr. Cook . . ."

"I'm sorry, Ellen, I forgot all about it."

"I just wanted to find out if you were all right."

"I'm fine."

"What'd you do to your arm?"

"I broke some ribs, but they'll be all right. Ribs usually heal pretty fast."

"Listen, Ben, I got a lotta loose ends to take care of, and I might as well do it now. But I'll get back to you later, believe me. Nice to see you again, Ellen. No, stay where you are, Ben. I can find my way out. I'm not completely helpless yet."

Ben took Chester's cup to the sink, because he didn't know what else to do with Ellen sitting there staring at him.

He felt old and tired and isolated. And there was nothing whatever that he wanted to say.

Maggie was vacuuming up above them, singing "Melancholy Baby." The wind was rushing around the back of the house while a pair of nuthatches fought against it, holding onto the bird feeder by the window above the sink.

"So Dr. Cook murdered Dr. West, and then murdered Miss Giardi?"

"Yes. Pathetic, isn't it? Ambition and envy being what they are."

"I think somebody ought to write about it. Sometime. I don't mean now, of course. Sort of a fictionalized account? Changing all the names, and using a different location?"

"You don't have anybody in mind, do you?" Ben looked at the straight black eyebrows wrinkling her forehead, and the blue eyes crinkled in concentration, and the soft lips pursed tightly together, and forced himself not to laugh. She was so intent, so caught up in what she was seeing in her own mind, while she stared out the window with her head tilted to one side.

"Would you tell me about it sometime? I don't want to pester you, Dr. Reese, it's just that knowing the people makes this much more interesting than if it were something I read about, that happened someplace else."

"Maybe. Sometime. What are you, a junior?"

"Yes."

Ben didn't want to spend the rest of that day alone, stuck with his own thoughts and his own losses. He'd rather take Ellen Winter somewhere. Out to see Journey maybe. And then into Columbus for dinner.

He also knew he wouldn't do it. Not when he was her professor and she was still an undergraduate.

"I was thinking, Ellen, that when you finish what you can do here on the coins, I can take the photographs with me when I go back to England, and do some of the legwork for you myself. It'll be easier than trying to do it by mail. Does that sound good, or would you rather I didn't?"

"No, that'd be great." She was looking at him skeptically.

It was almost like she'd had the feeling he wasn't going to say that at all, and had changed his mind at the last minute. And Ben did laugh, briefly, before his ribs made him catch his breath. "How would you feel about restoring a painting? I like the fact that it's more hands and less brain than the rest of what I do."

"Yeah, I'd like that. You mean now?"

"I have a portrait down in the basement we can start with, if you want to."

"Fine. Oh, before I forget. I saw Dr. Wingate on my way over, and he asked me to tell you he's sorry he didn't call back, but he's talked to Walter, whoever that is, and he wonders if you'd be willing to help him evaluate a horse he's found for his daughter."

"Ah! David *Wingate!*"

"Is it important?"

The phone rang and Ben stood there, staring at it. He let it ring three or four more times, but then he picked it up. He held it with his right shoulder and tried to adjust his other arm in the sling.

It was Mary Ann Cook again. And he didn't know what to say to her this time any more than he had the other times she'd called.

She actually didn't give him the opportunity to say much of anything. He just held the receiver against his ear and turned toward Ellen. He covered the mouthpiece and smiled self-consciously. And then he whispered very quietly, "This'll take a while, so help yourself to more coffee."

"Maybe I should go?"

"No, don't. But would you do me a favor and write me a note reminding me to call Richard's aunt?"

"Sure."

The pad was on the far side of the table, and Ellen pulled it over and reached for the pen, while Ben Reese listened to whoever was on the other end. He said, "I know," and "I'm sorry," and "If there's anything else I can do," as Ellen debated with herself, before giving in and reading the notes he'd already written:

- Invite Waldo Hubbard and wife to dinner if not well enough, take dinner there
- Pick up dissertation from Ed Campbell
- Do something for Jim's kids at Christmas presents and outing. Consider zoo?
- Remember to talk to Maggie about car

Ellen felt guilty immediately thereafter for prying into his private life. So she wrote the note and sipped her coffee and watched the birds on the feeder, while trying not to listen to anything else he said.

And yet when she turned back toward Ben, he looked so young, and so sad, and so patient, she would've liked to be able to ask him why.

But she couldn't. Not when he was her professor. And there was something self-contained about Ben Reese too, something that kept her from asking him things she might've asked someone else.

He'd been pacing slowly, four or five feet and back again. But then he stopped and muffled the mouthpiece with his good hand. "Remind me to ask Maggie how she'd feel about a dog."

"OK. I'll write you another note. What kind of dog?"

"Big. From the Humane Society." He sat down and tipped his chair back, before he took his hand off the receiver.

Ellen pushed his mug of coffee over to him, wondering how he'd gotten the scar, and where it went after it slid under his sleeve.

The employees of Thorndike Press hope you have enjoyed this Large Print book. All our Large Print titles are designed for easy reading, and all our books are made to last. Other Thorndike Press Large Print books are available at your library, through selected bookstores, or directly from us.

For information about titles, please call:

(800) 257-5157
To share your comments, please write:

Publisher
Thorndike Press
P.O. Box 159
Thorndike, Maine 04986